Praise

DIRECT THREAT will keep you on your toes trying to solve the mystery of who betrays who. Carissa, Frank, Marc, Kyle and Julie trust each other, but one of them masks murderous intentions. Olivia, the ten-year-old girl, is the prize some try to protect, and others try to betray. Follow the twists and turns of this exciting suspense as you enjoy the delight of newly discovered romance. Kimberly Rose Johnson has succeeded again in writing another compelling and unforgettable tale.

~Anne Greene, Award-winning author of Shadow of the Dagger,
CIA Operatives Book 1 and Red Is For Rookie, Book 1
in the Holly Garden PI Mystery series.

In Direct Threat, Kimberly Rose Johnson has created a book that will pull readers into a sweet romance laced with mystery and a dash of suspense. Sent to protect a child for the summer, Carissa Jones finds her heart opening to the child and to the possibility of love. But first she has to decide who to trust and who is the direct threat. A page turner that is perfect for a quick weekend read.

~Cara Putman, best-selling, award-winning author of
Flight Risk.

How does one start a protection service business? Two to begin and a third questionable hire. Throw-in a caterer and visiting friend. Guarding a ten-year-old shouldn't be a problem. Right? Add a budding romantic interest and things become confusing in a hurry. This book does not disappoint. Romance, adventure, and mystery. I look forward to book #2.

~*Linda Wood Rondeau Author of Second Helpings,*
a humorous contemporary novel.

"In her latest novel, Direct Threat, Kimberly Rose Johnson starts off with a bang. Literally! A suspenseful, faith-based story, complete with a clash of romance and treachery, you won't be disappointed with the first installment of this new series."

~ *C. Kevin Thompson, award-winning author of*
The Serpent's Grasp, The Blake Meyer Thriller series,
and The Letters

DIRECT THREAT

BY KIMBERLY ROSE JOHNSON

Direct Threat Published by Sweet Rose Press

This story is a work of fiction. All characters and events are the product of the author's imagination other than those stated in the author notes. Any other resemblance to any person, living or dead, is coincidental.

Scripture quotations are taken from the King James Version of the Bible. Public domain.

ISBN 978-0-9984315-7-4

Printed in the United States of America

Edited by Fay Lamb

1

Carissa Jones peered out of her client's front window. Unease settled in her stomach. The hair on her neck prickled. She pulled out her sidearm and looked toward the trees that edged the driveway. A branch wiggled back and forth as though it had been bumped. "Olivia! We need to go," Carissa called to the ten-year-old who'd been under her protection.

Olivia's mom rushed into the room and stopped. Her gaze rested on Carissa's Glock. Mrs. Drummond's skin faded a shade or two lighter. "Is it them?"

"I don't know for sure, but something feels wrong. Stay back and out of sight. I think someone's out there. Is Olivia packed?"

"Yes. She'll be down in a moment. Remember, Olivia thinks you're a family friend accompanying her to her grandparents for the summer. You're acting as her nanny while she's there. She is not to know about any of this. So put that thing away."

Keeping Olivia oblivious wasn't going to be easy,

but Carissa would do her best to honor the parents' wishes. "I understand." She holstered her weapon and turned from the window.

Glass shattered.

"Get down!" Carissa dove behind the couch. "Olivia go down the back stairs and meet us in the garage!" she shouted then called 9-1-1.

"Mom! Did you break something?" Olivia trotted down the stairs.

Carissa rose to protect the child, but Mrs. Drummond raced ahead to her daughter. "Everything's okay, sweetie. Didn't you hear Carissa tell you to go down the other stairs?" She looked wide-eyed at Carissa. With trembling hands she drew her daughter toward her.

Carissa waved her toward the back of the house, spoke softly to the dispatcher, and gave her clients an encouraging smile. She lowered the phone. "Hey, sweetie, how about you go and get in the car with your mom so we can head to the airport? I'll be there in a minute."

"Ok, but what about the window?"

"I'm talking with someone about the window right now," Carissa said. "Hurry. We don't want to miss the plane." She finished up with dispatch, ran to the back door, and grabbed her duffle off the counter as she passed.

A sinking feeling accompanied her into the garage. Her business partner, Frank Davis, would not be happy about this turn of events. This was supposed to be a simple assignment—escort a child to Oregon safely then be her bodyguard while staying on a well-secured estate. But simple didn't come close to describing the bullet lodged in the living room wall. Whoever had sent the threats to Olivia's parents meant business. They would have their hands full this summer if this was a sign of what was to come.

She hustled out to the garage where Mrs. Drummond sat behind the wheel. Carissa opened the driver's side door. "Change of plans. I'm driving, and you're sitting in back with Olivia."

"But—"

Carissa raised a brow.

The woman closed her mouth and stepped out.

"Thank you," Carissa said.

"Is it safe?" Mrs. Drummond whispered and blinked rapidly.

"Whoever was out there is probably long gone, but it's hard to say for certain." Carissa didn't believe in giving false hope. She kept her voice low, so Olivia wouldn't hear. "You hired Protection Inc. to keep your daughter safe for a reason—we're the best. But in order for me to do my job, I need to be in control and do things my way without you second-guessing or undermining me."

Mrs. Drummond nodded. Her fear-filled eyes indicated she wouldn't cross her—at least for now.

"The police are on their way. I'm sure whoever shot

at the house was only trying to scare us, or they would've hit someone." At least that's what she hoped.

Mrs. Drummond pursed her lips and slid in beside her daughter. "Olivia, do you remember a while back when your dad was really angry."

"Yes. I've never seen him like that."

"Well, there are some people who want to stop him from finishing the project he's working on. They must think that breaking our window will scare him into stopping work on his project, but that's not going to happen."

Carissa watched the ten-year-old in her rearview mirror. The girl's eyes widened, and she nodded.

"Is that why Carissa is going with me to Grandma and Grandpa's? I'm too old for a nanny."

"Yes. She'll watch out for you. But your grandparents are busy people so you *do* need a nanny. I expect you to listen to what Carissa tells you. Understood?"

"Yes, ma'am. Are we in danger right now?"

Mrs. Drummond's gaze met Carissa's.

"In order to keep you and your mom safe, I need to behave as though you are in danger." Carissa offered the mother and daughter an encouraging smile. "Buckle up and keep your heads down." Carissa hit the garage door opener and prayed no one was waiting on the other side. She threw the Mercedes into reverse, slammed her foot onto the accelerator then the brake, and swung the bulky car around in the oversized driveway.

Throwing the car into gear, she peeled out and raced down the long driveway. Trees and foliage on either side of the drive could be hiding the shooter. Her pulse thrummed in her ears. She narrowed her focus on the pavement ahead—*almost there.*

A shot ricocheted into the morning air.

Olivia screamed. "What was that?"

Mrs. Drummond whispered to the child, but Carissa couldn't understand her words. No matter—the bullet had missed them.

Carissa slammed the brakes but never completely stopped at the end of the drive. Fishtailing heavily, the car rounded onto the road. She steered into the slide and gained control. Accelerating again, she checked the mirrors—no one. They might make it to the airport in one piece yet.

Carissa kept a tight hold on Olivia's hand and walked with the herd of people exiting the secure area of the Portland, Oregon, airport. Her charge had grilled her incessantly on the flight about her driving skills. Olivia's parents might not want her to know Carissa's true job, but their daughter was smart. Before they'd landed, the girl had accused Carissa of being a stunt driver, a spy, a cop, and a racecar driver. The only thing she'd owned up to was being a cop once upon a time.

"Do you see my grandma and grandpa?" Olivia

craned her neck, walked on tiptoes, and looked from side to side. "There they are." She pointed to a couple who stood fifty feet away and picked up her pace.

Carissa wrapped her hand around the girl's forearm. "We need to stay together."

Olivia slowed. "Right. Sorry. I forgot."

A few feet from the grandparents, Carissa released her grip on the girl.

Olivia darted to the older couple who warmly embraced her. "Carissa used to be a cop, and she drives like they do in the movies."

Mr. Drummond chuckled. "Is that so?" He shot a disapproving look at Carissa as he shook her hand.

She grasped his firm grip.

"How was the flight?" he asked.

"Uneventful. Though the same couldn't be said for the trip to the airport."

"So I've gathered. My wife and I will take Olivia from here. We'll meet you at the house this evening."

"Of course." Carissa stepped back. "See you later, Olivia." She blended into the crowd but was never more than ten feet from her client. Whether her grandparents wanted to accept it or not, their granddaughter was in danger. At least it didn't appear they'd been tracked to the airport, but after the shooting, she couldn't be too careful.

A man approached the family from the west. Carissa went on alert. She didn't like Olivia being out in the open. She two-stepped to get closer to the girl. At the last moment, the man veered away from them. Carissa slowed.

Her phone buzzed. She tapped the device in her ear. "Frank. Speak to me." Her one-time partner with the Lincoln City Oregon Police Department and now co-owner of Protection Inc., chuckled.

"Always right to business. No hi, Frank. How are you? How's the weather?"

Carissa grinned at his teasing tone. "Hi, Frank. How are you? How was your drive from Seattle?"

"Not bad. I'm still on the road, arriving in Lincoln City shortly. From what I've heard, my day has been far less exciting than yours. I checked with Mrs. Drummond. Everyone there is fine, but whoever fired off the shots got away."

No surprise. "The senior Drummonds dismissed me until we get to their place on the coast."

"Tell me you're still tailing them."

"Give me some credit." Frank should know better than to ask a question like that. She took her job seriously at all times. This new assignment was unique though. They'd never been hired to protect a child, and she'd never played nanny to anyone. It should make for a rather interesting summer.

"Sorry. I know you too well to ask such a ridiculous question."

"Thank you." Carissa exited the airport and followed the family to short-term parking. She hoped they were headed straight to their home in Lincoln City.

Frank cleared his throat. ""Hello, CJ? You still there?"

"Sorry. Yes. I got distracted. What did you say?"

"I'm sending you a picture for where your car is parked. A key is under the back bumper."

She winced. Hopefully, the car was still there. She pulled her phone from her pocket and glanced at the photo. Should be easy enough to find.

Someone bumped her from behind. "Excuse me."

She whirled around and admired the well-built man who kept his focus on something ahead. "No problem." She followed his gaze and frowned. He looked way too interested in Olivia and her grandparents.

He stepped around her and continued forward. The man carried himself with a military bearing and no luggage. She quickened her steps.

"Everything okay?" Frank asked.

"Yes. Go on." She didn't let her focus stray from her client, but the military dude stuck close as though watching them, too. Senses on alert, she scanned the parking garage—no one stood out. She refocused her attention on military guy.

"After what happened, I arranged for Marc Olsen to help with protecting Olivia," Frank spoke into her ear. "We're going to have to step up the girl's protection detail over our original plan. As in around the clock."

"Wow. Okay." That wasn't good news, but she'd manage. "Marc Olsen's name is familiar, but I can't place him."

"An old friend. I probably mentioned him. He was my foster brother for a while. After what happened in Arizona, I'm not taking any chances."

She sighed. "Olivia is unharmed. I know how to do my job."

"Not suggesting you don't, but this case is more complicated than I was led to believe. We need him to help with the extra hours we'll be putting in."

"Fine, but in the future, I want a say in who we hire." They'd been in business together for the past year and had rapidly gained a good reputation as bodyguards in the Seattle area where they were based. "It's my reputation at stake, too."

"Understood. By the way, he's at the airport. I had him tail the Drummonds from their home on the coast."

"You could have opened with that." He's either exceptional at not being noticed, or he lost them. Military man still hung close enough to make her wonder if that could be Marc. "Can you send me a picture of our new guy?"

Silence

"Hello? Frank?" She looked at the screen. The call dropped. She had no idea if the man who appeared to be tailing the Drummonds was friend or foe and didn't have time to call Frank back to find out—time was of the essence. "Excuse me, sir."

He looked back with a frown but quickly turned his attention to her client and quickened his pace.

She chased after him. "Hey, stop."

He looked over his shoulder and stopped.

Unable to slow fast enough, Carissa sprinted headlong into the man's backside. The force of the impact knocked him off balance. He tripped and their feet tangled. He fell, taking her with him. *Oof.* Air whooshed from her lungs. Pain shot up her arms as she collapsed onto his back.

Stunned, she didn't move for a few seconds. "So sorry. I didn't think you'd stop like that." She scooted off of him. Why hadn't she zigged or zagged?

He raised his head slightly then rolled over and stood. "You said to stop." He rubbed his shoulder.

"True." Had she injured him? He'd apparently managed to break their fall with his hands because his handsome face was unharmed. She watched her client round the corner at the end of the row.

He glanced toward the parking garage and sighed before turning back to her. "Are you okay?"

"Other than feeling a little foolish, I'm fine. I'm sorry about barreling into you. I really didn't mean to cause you to fall."

He waved off her apology. "Now that you have my attention, what did you want?"

She cleared her throat. "Oh. Uh...I thought you were someone else. Excuse me." She darted in the direction of her car. If she hurried, she'd still be able to tail the Drummonds.

Marc Olsen frowned after the brunette who looked to be in her late twenties, about five foot eight, one hundred fifty pounds, and fit. But he had no time to push her for answers. He'd lost his client and had to find her fast. He couldn't let Frank down.

Adrenalin surged, pushing him to run hard for his vehicle, then tear out of the garage with squealing tires. He had to locate the couple he'd followed from Lincoln City. Frank said to tail them everywhere they went until they returned to town. So far, he'd lost them twice. Once at the airport when a sea of bodies caused him to lose visual on the couple at the same time they'd acquired the child in their care. Too bad Frank hadn't filled him in on the full scope of this job. It had been very last minute, but since he and Frank had history, he'd agreed.

All he knew was that he wasn't to lose the older couple. Good thing Frank wasn't privy to his current situation. With any luck, he'd find the silver BMW the older couple drove and see them safely home. After that, he was supposed to meet up with Frank and his business partner, CJ.

He kept on alert for the couple he was supposed to be tailing. He never imagined his stint as an Army MP would one day qualify him to be a bodyguard. At least that was the idea. He slammed his palm against the steering wheel. Where had they gone?

A flash of silver caught his attention. "Bingo." He accelerated then followed the BMW at a discreet distance and settled deeper into the seat. A car coming up behind him wove through traffic much like a racecar driver. He gripped the steering wheel harder. Marc straightened as the reckless driver whipped past him. The car bounded forward and closed in on the Drummonds. His heart thrummed wildly, and he accelerated.

He would not fail his first assignment.

2

Carissa stood with Frank and former colleague, John, a few feet inside John's condo. She and Frank had worked with John when they were employed by the Lincoln City PD. He was the reason they were on the case. He'd heard about the situation with the Drummonds and recommended their services.

A knock on the door drew their attention. John pulled it open. "You must be Marc."

"That'd be me."

"Come in. Your team is waiting."

His gaze landed on Carissa. The man's brown eyes held confusion. "What's going on?" He looked at Frank.

"This is my business partner, CJ."

Carissa offered a grin. "Hi, again."

He crossed his arms, causing his biceps to bulge. "I don't understand. Why did you—?"

"Frank neglected to give me a description of our new hire." She shrugged. "And I go by Carissa." Though she trusted Frank with her life, his communication skills were lacking. He could have, at the very least, sent a photo of Marc so they could have been working together rather than against one another. But she had to admit the man knew how to pick good help.

Marc rubbed the back of his neck. "When Frank said CJ was his former partner with the PD, I assumed you were a man."

She shrugged. "He has a problem with names." She looked pointedly at Frank as he guided them toward the kitchen.

Frank smacked his chewing gum. "Sorry 'bout that. You know you'll always be CJ to me. I can't help it if people assume you're a man."

She pushed down her frustration and turned her attention back to Marc. "You've been briefed?"

Marc nodded. "We're guarding a ten-year-old girl while she visits her grandparents for the summer. Her dad is a scientist working on a highly sensitive project."

Frank rubbed his chin as he looked back and forth between the two of them. "Correct. John here will assist us if we need any extra help."

John nodded. "I'll jump in whenever and wherever I'm needed. I went to high school with Olivia's dad and promised him Frank and Carissa were the best."

Carissa grinned. She had always liked John.

"Thanks for the endorsement," Frank said "Shortly before CJ and Olivia left Phoenix, someone fired on them. Our intel had suggested she might be grabbed and held for ransom. This latest development came as a surprise."

Carissa watched Marc closely. Would he back down and decide being a bodyguard wasn't for him? Was he really ready to put his life on the line for a child? Clearly, he was willing to die for his country, but this was different.

Marc raised his chin.

Frank continued. "We don't believe Olivia was tracked here, but we do anticipate she'll be found eventually. This goes without saying, but be vigilant. I called in a favor with another buddy at the local PD. He's keeping an eye on the family until we're set up at the estate. I e-mailed the rotation schedule to each of you."

Carissa pulled two sheets of paper from her oversized bag. "Sorry, John. I didn't think to print one for you since you're not in the rotation. I saw the e-mail and printed a hard copy for each of us." She handed one to Frank and another to Marc. His fingers brushed hers, shooting a tingle up her arm. She caught her breath. The man had an effect on her she didn't welcome. A child's life was in the balance, and she needed to focus.

"We'll work in eight-hour shifts," Frank continued.

Marc studied the schedule. "Looks good to me. So what's with this kid? I get her dad is some big-time scientist, but why is his daughter in danger?" He pulled up one of the barstools to the large granite kitchen counter.

Frank cleared his throat. "I thought you read the case file."

Marc raised his chin slightly. "It didn't state why we're protecting the girl."

Frank nodded. "A group wants what her dad is working on. He's received death threats. A specific threat against his daughter was made, alluding to her safety if he didn't give them what they wanted. Based on what happened at their home earlier today, I'm inclined to believe that threat is real."

Marc blew out a slow breath. "Who's watching out for the parents?"

"Not our purview. We were hired specifically to make sure their daughter remains safe."

"Understood," Marc said.

Frank gave him a look of approval.

John handed them each glasses filled with ice water. "Fortunately, a plan was already in place to move Olivia to Lincoln City for the summer with her grandparents. They want her to spend time with them away from the stress of their lives." He sipped his water. "After the attack at their house, it appears to be a prudent move. I'm glad he confided his situation to me. There's no way I could have handled her protection detail on my own."

Carissa shifted the cold glass to her other hand. "We appreciate the business. Not that we didn't have enough in Seattle, but it's nice to come back here for the summer." It had been a while since either of them had been in Lincoln City. When Frank had presented her with his idea of Protection Inc.,they'd moved fast and hadn't been back since. "We'll do our best to not let you down, John."

"I appreciate that, and I know Olivia's dad does, too."

Marc sipped the water. "Poor kid. So we're Olivia's new safety net."

Carissa studied their new hire—at least six foot with broad shoulders and a trim waistline. A strong jawline and a five o'clock shadow complimented the I-just-crawled-out-of-bed hairstyle he sported. His military training was an asset. He was perfect on paper and in person, but something about him bothered her. "Do you have any experience with kids, Marc? Ten-year-old girls in particular?"

"Not much, but I figure they're like anyone else, just smaller."

Carissa grinned. "Right." She dragged out the word.

Unease filled Marc. He didn't know the first thing about pre-teen girls. When Frank had called him earlier today and asked him to join his team, he'd assumed they'd be guarding a stalking victim. A kid had never crossed his mind. "When do we meet up with the client?"

Frank glanced at his watch. "About an hour. You sure you're up for this, Marc?"

"Absolutely." The idea that someone had

threatened a little girl didn't sit well, and he'd do everything in his power to make sure she stayed safe.

Carissa pulled up the case file on her laptop and turned the screen toward him. "This will tell you all we know. Oh, and one more thing—Olivia can't know we're her bodyguards. Due to the attack on their home in Phoenix, she strongly suspects there's more to me than simply being her nanny, but the less she knows about the two of you the better."

"Seriously?" This was more complicated than he'd imagined. "How is that supposed to work?"

Frank cleared his throat. "The child was told friends of CJ are visiting for the summer. We'll occupy the guesthouse. I'll enter the house after she goes to bed." Frank glanced at his watch again. "I have a stop to make before we assemble at the estate. I'll meet you both there."

Marc nodded and stared at the computer screen. When he'd joined the Army ten years ago, he never imagined a future as a bodyguard. Life had taken some unexpected twists, not necessarily bad ones, but definitely not planned.

"You ready to head out?" Carissa finished off her water then placed the cup in the sink.

"Guess so." This woman intrigued him. Frank had filled him in somewhat about their story, but the soft look in her green eyes didn't fit with the tough persona she projected. From what Frank said, she was a crack shot, and he could trust her with his life.

Carissa closed the laptop and slid it into a computer case. "Thanks for bringing my stuff with you, Frank. The overnight bag I packed before flying to Phoenix is fine for a weekend, but a girl needs some of her favorite things."

Frank chuckled. "Your fancy espresso machine is still in the trunk of my car. I'll keep it in the guesthouse if that's okay with you."

"That would probably be best. I'm glad you drove rather than flew, so I didn't have to live without my favorite life accessory. Thanks for picking it up for me." She looked at Marc. "After you see this place, you'll wish our job was longer than the summer. From the pictures I've seen, the guesthouse is beyond comfortable, and the main house is a mansion." She scribbled an address on a sticky note and handed it to him. "We're due there in a little less than an hour. Don't be late."

"Got it. I'll go check out of my hotel." He'd booked a room when Frank had called, not realizing they'd be living at the estate.

Carissa shrugged on a lightweight sweater that covered the 9mm at her waist.

Marc waved and sauntered out. He hopped into his 4x4 pickup and turned the key. The engine roared to life. Ah, he loved that sweet purr. He shifted into gear.

Carissa had been a surprise, more than just the fact she was a woman rather than a dude like he'd thought. She was attractive, and her feisty personality only added to the attraction. He sure hadn't expected that. Hopefully, he hadn't offended her, especially since they'd be living so close for the next three months. Now to prove himself capable. The only problem…he'd never been a bodyguard. But how hard could it be to protect a ten-year-old girl?

Standing on the edge of the cliff, bordering the property, Carissa looked out over the Pacific. Frank stood beside her. Wind whipped her hair, irritating her eyes. She slipped a hair band off her wrist and pulled her hair into a ponytail. She checked her watch for the third time in twenty minutes. "You sure about the new guy? He's late."

"Of course. He'll be here," Frank said.

"What made you hire him?"

"I trust him, and I knew he was available."

"I remember you telling me about some of your earlier exploits with him. You sure he's reformed?" Frank had mentioned the foster brother he'd gotten into trouble with as a teen—not bad trouble, only stupid stuff like skipping school.

"Of course. This is important to me, CJ. Marc's floundered since leaving the military. He needs this, and we need him. Trust me. He's going to be a great addition to our company." He looked at her expectantly. "What do you think of him so far?"

She sucked in a breath. "I think he's late."

Frank's forehead scrunched. "I'll talk to him about that when he gets here, but I'm sure he has a good reason for being late."

"I hope so." She might be a tad obsessive about being on time.

"Marc's a bachelor."

She chuckled. "I sure hope that's not his excuse for being late." Although it might be why he's single. She glanced at her watch again.

"Not what I was getting at. I thought maybe when this case is over, if the two of you hit it off, you might ask him out."

"Please. I can't believe we're having this conversation. Why are you always so concerned with my love life?"

"It's your lack of one that has me concerned. You've been cranky."

She laughed. She was not cranky—well at least not most of the time. Right now her patience had worn thin. "My lack of a life outside of work is why I can do what we do. Besides, you don't have a life either, and you're ten years older than me."

"The right woman hasn't come along," he muttered.

"As if you'd ever have time to meet her if she did." She rolled her eyes. "The only way you'll ever meet a woman is if she's one of our clients, because all we ever do is work. How many jobs did you turn down so we could spend the summer here?"

"No comment."

"Exactly, and for the record, I'm glad we're here. It's nice to be back in our old stomping grounds. I won't miss Seattle for a minute," Carissa said.

"Come to think of it, neither will I. Remind me again why we decided to base our business there."

"Plenty of work." She smirked.

"Right." He chuckled. Then he looked toward the property's gate. Concern etched his face. "Give Marc a chance. I really think the two of you—"

"Frank…" she dragged out his name with a warning tone. He'd learned early on how to push her buttons and took great pleasure in doing so. Regardless, she loved him like a dad. Sure, he looked rough around the edges and acted gruff, but it was an act perfected from years as an undercover vice cop. Inside, a big teddy bear lurked.

"Relax, CJ. I'm only messing with you."

Crunching gravel drew her attention, and a black 4x4 parked next to her car. A smile tugged at her lips, and she quickly erased it.

Frank blew out a breath. "'Bout time."

A minute later, Marc sidled up alongside them. "Wow! What a view. I could get used to this."

"You're late." She crossed her arms.

"Yeah, sorry. I asked for directions at the hotel, and they were less than helpful. I ended up in Salishan before I realized I'd missed my turn."

Carissa shot Frank a look. Had Marc unwittingly

put Olivia in danger by giving away his location? Not likely, since they'd have to know he was protecting the girl, but one could never be too careful in their line of work. A slip of the tongue could be a matter of life or death, and she was in no hurry to see heaven. "Glad you made it back."

As soon as Olivia arrived, they'd be in business. The Drummonds had called a bit ago to say they'd be there soon. She didn't like that they were depending on someone else to watch the family right now, but some things couldn't be helped. She checked her watch again. A knot in her stomach grew tighter. The front gate swung open, and the couple's BMW drove onto the estate.

Finally.

3

Carissa, flanked by Marc and Frank, stood near the rock garden that separated the main house from the guesthouse, along with Olivia and her grandparents. Carissa looked down at the girl, smiled, and offered a fist bump. "We're going to have so much fun this summer."

Olivia giggled. "Our rooms are right next to each other, just like at my house." She eyed the large men standing beside Carissa and fidgeted with the hem of her top.

"I know." Carissa snagged Marc and Frank by their arms. "These are friends of mine. Marc and Frank are joining us for the summer."

"Okay." Olivia looked up at her grandmother. "Can we eat now? I'm starving."

Linda Drummond patted her shoulder. "Of course." She turned to the men. "Are you settled in the guesthouse?"

"Yes, thank you," Frank said.

"Carissa, I trust you've already eaten?" Linda raised her brows.

Seemed the woman was laying some ground rules, but Carissa had a job to do whether Grandma liked it or not. "Actually, no. Do you mind if I join you?" The older woman needed to understand she would be her granddaughter's shadow.

Linda gave a weak smile. "Of course not, dear."

"Thanks. I'll be right behind you."

Their clients walked toward the main house but not before Olivia asked why the scary looking old guy looked so grumpy. Carissa missed their reply. She covered her mouth with her hand to hide a smile.

"Who is she calling old?" Frank puffed out his chest.

Marc slapped him on the back. "That's not the important part. She thinks you're scary."

"Get a haircut and shave, Frank." Carissa tossed over her shoulder.

"I look fine."

She shook her head. "In Olivia's world, you resemble a thug. Try looking like one of the good guys for a few months."

Frank groaned, and Marc let out a hearty laugh. She glanced over her shoulder and locked eyes with Marc. Catching her breath, she whirled and faced forward. Carissa double-timed it to catch up to the family. No way would she allow *his* rugged good looks to distract her from her job.

Marc's brows rose. What was that look on the boss lady's face? It intrigued him, much like the woman herself.

"We better get settled and grab a bite before you're on duty. CJ needs time alone with the family to work her magic. Then you'll take over." Frank sauntered to the guesthouse, and Marc walked beside him.

"Work her magic?"

"Did you notice how hostile the grandmother was?"

"Kind of impossible to miss."

Frank unlocked the door and stepped inside. "She doesn't want us here. But her husband and son, Olivia's dad, won the battle. Linda believes Olivia's safe and not in any real danger. She's unaware of the shooting earlier today, and her daughter-in-law doesn't want her to know. Thinks it will freak her out." He flipped on an overhead fan. "Linda resents our intrusion in her life."

It seemed Carissa had multiple talents. "I hope Carissa is successful, or this will be a very long summer."

Frank brushed past him into the small kitchen. "You catch on fast. Knew there was a reason I hired you, since it wasn't for your sense of direction or discretion." A look of annoyance crossed his face. He pulled two cans of soda from the fridge, slid one across the counter, and took a drink from his own.

"Sorry I was late." Marc popped the lid. Clearly, Frank was irritated. Talk about a rough first day. He was under no illusion that their past history would keep him employed. He had to prove himself, or he'd be looking for a job—again.

"You never should've given away your location to the person at the hotel. You ever heard of GPS? It's included with your phone."

Marc tensed. "I'm aware. It was a slipup. It won't happen again."

"See that it doesn't."

"What's going on, Frank? Do you regret hiring me? If you want, I'll quit. I'm sure John would be willing to step in for me."

"Simmer down, little brother. CJ thinks I made a mistake in hiring you. I don't like being wrong."

Marc stared at the half-empty soda. He owed Frank more than the man realized. Had it not been for Frank and Frank's family, Marc would probably be dead. He'd been close to ending it all when he'd been moved to their home at the age of fourteen. His time with them had changed his life. His only regret was skipping one too many classes together and getting removed from their home.

"You weren't wrong about me." Since leaving the military, he'd done odd jobs. The time had come to dig in and prove he was worth the risk. "I'll be the best bodyguard you've ever worked with."

A cross between a chuckle and a choke erupted

from Frank's mouth. "We'll see 'bout that. Just stay alert, and instinct will do the rest."

"Mind if I ask you something?"

"No."

"Why'd you hire me? I've never been a bodyguard."

"Because I know you." Frank pulled a bag of frozen burgers from the freezer and placed two on a plate. "Seems to me you're like this patty—raw and untried. I'm going to take this out to the grill, season it, and let it cook slowly until it's the way I like. I prefer to prepare my own meat. That way it turns out just right. If someone else makes it, then I'll have to re-do it to my taste. You follow?"

"You hired me because of my inexperience?"

Frank walked out to the back patio. "Don't worry about CJ. I trained her, too. She's one of the best."

Carissa slipped out the front door and breathed in the salty air. She slid on a windbreaker and sauntered to the cliffside overlooking the Pacific Ocean. The sun, low over the horizon, held her captive for a moment. She never tired of watching the sunset.

Marc stood by the stairs leading down to the beach. He waved and meandered over to her. The breeze ruffled his dark hair, and his lips curved into a smile. He still sported the five o'clock shadow, but now it had filled in a little more.

Under any other circumstances this would feel like a romantic interlude, but it wasn't, and she needed to keep her head in the game. Distractions could be disastrous.

"The cameras are all working, and the gate is secure." Marc nodded toward the beach. "Looks like this is the weak spot."

"I agree. I don't like the vulnerability, but short of fencing off the cliff and installing a locked gate, there's nothing we can do except be vigilant. Anyone trying to get to Olivia will have to go through me first." There was a reason she would be in the room next to the girl.

Marc nodded. "Anything I should know?"

"Yeah. The house is palatial with lots of open space, and the floors are all Travertine tile. The art work is impressive, and the view of the ocean, show-stopping."

"You trying to make me jealous?"

"No, just thought you'd want to know that footsteps are easily heard. There's a lot of glass facing the ocean, and it's an art thief's dream house."

"Noted."

Carissa turned. "'Night, Marc. And, in case I neglected to say it earlier, welcome aboard." She turned, but not before his eyes widened and a lazy smile lit his face. Too bad they were working. She'd finally met a man who didn't seem intimidated by what she did for a living. Maybe Frank had been onto something after all.

4

A week later, Carissa slipped off her shoes when she and Olivia reached the white sand at the bottom of the stairs. She lifted her left shoe and examined it for a moment, playing with the sole, where she always had a bulge.

"Something wrong?" Olivia asked.

Carissa held her shoes with one hand and shielded her eyes, studying the people on the beach. "Nope. Just checking out something." What caused the slight bulge in her shoe would remain Carissa's secret.

A few runners, taking advantage of the low tide, passed by on the shoreline. A boy and man flew a dragon kite that probably could have taken the child for a ride without the man's help. Several people strolled near the waves, but no one made her nervous.

Olivia grabbed her hand and tugged. "Come on, CJ. I want to see the tide pools."

Carissa ran alongside the girl. Olivia had used her nickname since she'd overheard Frank call her CJ. The girl was nice, despite her high-end fashion and obsession with everything Hollywood. If she had to predict the child's future, she'd say Olivia would either be a movie star or a film director. "Slow down. The tide pool isn't going anywhere soon. Look how far out the water is."

"I know, but Mom and Dad never take me to the beach to play."

She chuckled. "That's probably because you live in a land-locked state."

"I can't believe Grandma didn't mind us coming down here." She turned and waved to Linda who stood cliffside at the top of the stairs. "I'm glad you're visiting this summer. I don't need a nanny, but I'd be so bored without you here." She pulled out her phone and snapped a picture of a nearby seagull.

Carissa chuckled. "Thanks, but I'm sure you'd find something to do." Surprisingly, Olivia wasn't addicted to her phone unless taking pictures and recording video counted.

"Maybe, but it's more fun with you."

Touched beyond words, Carissa swallowed hard and pushed down the lump that formed in her throat. "Race you!" She took off at half speed not waiting for a response, knowing Olivia would be on her heels.

"No fair! You got a head start."

Carissa anticipated the girl's movements and made the race a tie. "You're fast."

"Thanks." Olivia pointed to the stairs leading up to their house. "Isn't that Marc?"

Carissa turned. "Sure is. He's early." Hopefully, they hadn't encountered a problem. She checked her cell for missed messages and found none.

"It's never too early to play on the beach." Olivia squatted beside the tide pool.

"I suppose you're right." Carissa pointed to a sand crab. "Look."

"I like the ones with pretty shells best."

Carissa's cell phone vibrated in her pocket. A glance at the screen brought a grin to her face. "Hi, Julie. What's up?" They'd been friends for years and had spent many hours on a beach not far from here looking for shells or surfing.

"I was calling to ask you the same thing. I thought we were having lunch today."

"Oh, no. I completely forgot." Carissa looked up and down the beach for trouble. No bystanders looked out of place or suspicious. A girl about Olivia's age knelt beside her and started talking. Carissa tuned out their conversation and stepped further from the children. "I know I set up our lunch, but I'm on a case that's turned out to be bigger than I'd expected. I'll be working almost 24/7 for the entire summer. I'm sorry."

"Seriously? That stinks. I was hoping we could go surfing sometime, like we did in the old days."

Carissa focused on the crashing waves for a moment then shook her head. "I'm really sorry. My days of surfing are over, at least for the present."

"I miss my old friend. What did you do with her?"

"She grew up. How about I call you when I've settled into a routine? We'll do coffee or something."

"Sure. That sounds good. Are you on the beach? I hear the surf."

"Yes, but I'm working."

"Okay. Call me when you can."

"Will do. Thanks for understanding." Carissa pocketed her cell and returned to Olivia's side. Guilt for standing up her longtime friend made her stomach upset. She'd have to make it up to her. She looked down at the girl. "What do you have there?"

Olivia held up a snail-like shell. "I don't know, but it's cool. Can I keep it?"

"Sorry, no. There's a live creature in there. It'd die if you took it home."

Olivia's eye widened. "I didn't know." She set the snail back where she'd found it.

Carissa waved to Marc.

He lifted a hand and jogged toward them.

Olivia picked her way across the exposed sand and rocks toward the girl that looked to be close to Olivia's age and presumably the girl's mother. Watching Olivia with the other girl reminded her of when she and Julie would go to the beach as teens. They'd spent hours surfing and hanging out with friends. She'd lost touch with most of her high school classmates, but Julie had stuck—mostly. They'd drifted apart since she'd become a bodyguard.

Marc walked up beside her. "How's it going?"

She shook off the melancholy and grinned. "The sky is blue, the sun is shining, and there's a slight breeze. About perfect if you ask me."

"Who's the woman with Olivia and that girl?" Marc spoke out of the side of his mouth.

"I think it's the girl's mom, but I'll find out for sure." Carissa approached the trio and rested a hand on Olivia's shoulder. "She just loves these tide pools. Looks like your daughter does, too."

"Yes. Stephanie's into sea creatures. We went to the aquarium in Newport yesterday. Have you been?"

"Not yet. Are you staying in Lincoln City?"

"Yes. We're visiting from Washington for the week."

"Enjoy your stay." Carissa gently squeezed Olivia's shoulder. "Time to go."

The girl's head dipped. "Fine." She kicked her bare feet through the sand. "Why'd we have to leave? That's the first girl my age I've seen."

Carissa laughed. "You've been here all of a week."

"So." She crossed her arms.

"I don't know about you ladies," Marc rubbed his stomach, "but I could use some ice cream."

"Yeah! Hey, there's Grandma." Olivia sprinted toward Linda who watched from her perch on a large weathered log near the stairs that led up to their estate.

Carissa and Marc ran after the girl but stopped a few feet away.

Olivia plopped onto her knees. "Grandma, can I get ice cream with Marc and CJ?"

Marc nudged Carissa in the side with his elbow. "How come the kid can call you CJ and I can't."

Carissa lowered her voice. "Olivia can call me whatever she wants. Nice save with the ice cream. I thought we might come to blows for a minute."

"You could've taken her." He winked then turned his attention back to their client.

A shiver shot through Carissa. She was way too attracted to this man.

Linda and Olivia walked back toward the stairs, the spring in Olivia's step missing.

"Looks like ice cream is out," Carissa whispered and followed at a discreet distance. "What are you doing down here anyway?"

"Thought I'd take a jog before going on duty. Frank's watching the monitors. So far, everything's quiet."

"Good. Let's hope it stays that way." She'd like to believe it would be an easy summer, but instinct told her, they were in for a rough ride. She noticed his athletic shorts and tank for the first time. "Enjoy your workout."

"Plan to. See you in a bit."

Carissa half-wanted to join him. Although running wasn't a pleasure, doing so with Marc would enjoyable, and she needed to keep in shape for the occasional client who ran. She'd learned that lesson the hard way when someone she'd once guarded had set out for a two-mile jog.

She prayed this would be a quiet summer, and Linda would be proven right. She'd hate for Olivia to be exposed again to anyone intent on hurting her or her family.

Marc adjusted course and headed away from the crashing waves. So far, being a bodyguard was a lot easier than he expected. Aside from when he was on duty, his time was his own. All he had to do was shadow the girl until her bedtime then watch the security monitors until Frank took over. Granted, Carissa was on pretty much 24/7, which made his and Frank's jobs much easier.

True to his word, Frank had been molding him into a bodyguard. Sometime since high school, Frank had found God, and He was a big part of who Frank was now. Marc respected that, but he wasn't one to wear his religion on his sleeve.

The thing he found most troublesome was that Frank prayed God would help them keep the girl safe. Now, Marc knew God loved them, but He had a big world to take care of with a lot of major problems. Why would He care about one little girl when she had three people watching out for her day and night?

Maybe he should bring this up with Carissa. She might be able to explain what the deal was with Frank since they'd worked together for so long. The tide had begun to come in, so he did an about-face. Time to head back and shower.

A few hours later, Marc walked along the perimeter of the property. Buzzing bees broke through the distant sound of the surf. A car approached, and the gate opened. Linda's BMW pulled in. He spotted Carissa getting out of the front seat of Linda's sedan. He walked toward the driveway. Carissa waved to him and said something to the duo. She strode toward him. "How's it going?"

"Quiet."

"Good. That's exactly what we want. What's Frank doing?" she asked.

"Sleeping."

Carissa sighed. "Guess I'll stay close to Olivia until she's in bed. You can continue to monitor the grounds. I thought this eight-hour shift thing would work, but so far it's failed miserably."

For the first time, he really looked at her face and noticed the telltale signs of fatigue. "You getting burned out?"

"I'm fine. Just not used to keeping up with a ten-year-old." Dark circles shaded her eyes.

"Are you sleeping okay?" Concern for her welfare hit him. He hadn't even thought about the toll this case had on her. Sure, she was the boss, but he couldn't help worrying about her. He'd step it up and try to ease her burden.

She shrugged. "You know how it is sleeping in a

new bed and adjusting to the sounds of a different house. I brought my own quilt to help me sleep, but I'm always listening for any hint of trouble from Olivia's room."

"Makes me think Frank and I are lucky to be in the guesthouse. I could come relieve you sooner in the day. You don't have to be with Olivia all the time. That would give you a chance to get out of here and take a break."

"Thanks." She touched his forearm. "That's really nice of you. I might take you up on that."

"Good. It's so quiet. Why don't you cut out now? I can handle things."

"It's tempting, but I want to run this past Frank first." She looked over her shoulder and lowered her voice. "I can't blow my cover with Olivia. She thinks I'm her nanny and, as such, I'm pretty much a constant in her life. If you stepped in all of a sudden…"

"I understand." They meandered to the stone bench near the front door of the main house and sat. Marc kept his voice low. "How's it going with Linda? Is she still resisting us?"

"At times, but for the most part, she's treating me like one of the family. Olivia's an absolute sweetie, but she's quite the drama queen. I predict a future in Hollywood for that girl."

"I suppose there are worse things she could do." He looked toward the closed gate at the driveway.

"Like what?"

"I don't know." He grinned. "Be a bodyguard."

Carissa playfully slugged him in the shoulder.

"Ouch." He rubbed the spot. She hadn't really hit him hard, and it was worth it to see a smile light her eyes. "That wasn't necessary."

"Yes, it was."

A white van stopped at the gate.

Her eyes narrowed. "Looks like we have unexpected company."

Marc bolted to standing. "I'll check it out."

Carissa grabbed Marc's wrist. "Hold on a sec." They shouldn't draw attention to themselves. If the van held an enemy, she wanted the element of surprise. But if someone was lost, there was no need to cause a scene. "I'm going to slip inside. Stay out of sight, and keep an eye on the van."

Carissa followed the sound of Olivia's giggles. She breezed into the library and spotted Linda on the couch next to her granddaughter. Olivia and her grandmother each held a book.

"Excuse me, Linda. May I have a word?"

Linda must have sensed the urgency, because she immediately stood and followed Carissa to the front door. "What's wrong?"

"Maybe nothing. There's a white van at the front gate. Are you expecting anyone?"

"No. And no one buzzed the house either."

"Okay."

"What should I do?"

"Keep Olivia in the library. I'll let you know when all is clear."

Linda nodded and nearly flew back to the young girl's side.

A knock at the door drew Carissa's attention. She gripped her Glock. "Who is it?"

"Marc."

She returned her pistol to its holster, unlocked, and opened the door.

Marc slipped inside. "I waited for a while, but when the van continued to sit there, I approached it. The driver reversed and peeled out."

She clenched and unclenched her fingers. "I told you to stay out of sight. Never mind. Go wake Frank and fill him in. Meet me here when you're done." Had Olivia's location been compromised?

"You look angry." Marc's tone held surprise. "I know what you said, but you weren't there, and you can't expect me to just stand there and not do something. I'm in this, too, you know. I care about what happens to Olivia."

"Are you finished?" Carissa took several calming breaths.

"Yes." He raised his chin and turned toward the guesthouse.

Maybe she'd been too hard on him. But she'd told

him what she wanted him to do, and last she checked she was still the boss. She whirled around and strode into the family room.

Linda arched her brow as Olivia sat clueless beside her.

Carissa forced a smile, hoping to convey that the immediate danger had passed. "I'll be back in a bit."

Olivia looked up from the book her grandmother held. "This is a great story, CJ. You'd like it. It's about a horse called Candlelight."

"I love horses." Frank and Marc could wait a minute or two since the danger had passed—for now. Besides, if she didn't take a minute with the child, Olivia would know something was up. The last thing she wanted was to upset Olivia. She stepped across the room and sank beside the girl. "May I see?"

Olivia flipped the book closed and pointed to the horse on the cover. "That's Candlelight."

Carissa turned the book over and read the blurb on the back. "Maybe I'll borrow it sometime. Sounds like something I'd like. I'm going to go visit my friends in the guesthouse."

"May I come? I've never seen the guesthouse."

Carissa's brows rose, and she caught the slight shake of Linda's head. "I'm sorry, sweetie. The men have turned it into a man cave. I don't think you'd like it. I won't be long." She tapped the girl's nose. "Besides, you and your grandma are still reading." She stood. "Sorry for interrupting."

"That's okay." Olivia snuggled up against the side of the couch and began reading again.

Carissa turned and strode to the entryway as the lock on the front door turned.

Frank entered with Marc close behind.

"I was headed over to see you," Carissa greeted.

Frank nodded toward the study and settled at the desk with his computer. He opened his laptop and kept his voice low. "I downloaded the footage of the gate for the past five minutes." He pressed play.

Carissa peered close at the image on the screen, unable to make out the driver. Marc's breath warmed her neck as he peered over her shoulder. She shouldn't have been so short with him. They needed someone who had initiative when no one was around—someone who could think for himself and not need to be told every little thing.

"Can you zoom in on the driver's face?" Marc brushed against her shoulder.

"I wish, but we don't have that kind of technology." Frank pointed to where the license plate should've been. "Plate's missing." The scene continued to play, and the van took off. "This must be when the driver spotted you. Did you get an impression of what he was up to?"

"I think I startled him." Marc said. "I didn't get a good look at his face. He wore shades and his hair was dark."

"At least we have something. Good job." Frank replayed the video again. "Okay. Let's assume the van was a threat. From now on, no less than two of us will be on duty at all times. Carissa, you've had a long day. I'll take over for now. You look like you haven't slept in a while. Get some rest."

Carissa propped her hands on her waist. "I'll stay with Olivia as usual until she goes to bed at eight. You can relieve me then." What was it with these guys? Didn't they know better than to tell a woman she looked bad? Sure, she was tired, but no less than Frank, judging by his bloodshot eyes. If anyone needed sleep, he did.

Frank raised his hands in surrender. "I know better than to argue when you stand like that."

Carissa lowered her hands to her side and held back a grin. This was why they made a great team. Frank knew how to diffuse her ire.

"You're not going to take me up on my offer either?" Marc asked.

"Not tonight. I want to stay with Olivia."

"Because of the van?" A knowing look filled Marc's eyes. It seemed he could read her mind.

She nodded. "For what it's worth, you did the right thing approaching the van. I'm sorry I snapped."

He raised his brows. "Thanks. How much longer do you suppose Olivia will go to bed at eight willingly? I used to stay up until ten during the summer. Drove my parents nuts."

Carissa squeezed her eyes shut then blinked a few times. A later bedtime would be a problem. She'd have to talk to Linda and let her know they needed to keep the strict bedtime.

They finished their meeting then went their separate ways.

Carissa shot an arrow prayer to God for the safety of her team and the girl in their care. A flash in her mind of the night that changed her life made her shoulders tense. She couldn't help but compare herself to Olivia. They were both ten when evil invaded their innocent lives. But if she did her job right, Olivia would never experience the trauma she and her mother had.

"CJ, why are you in the hallway?" Olivia stood a few feet from her with her hip thrust to the side. She rested one hand at her waist and the other was extended palm up.

Carissa grinned at the dramatic pose. "I was thinking about being ten." She turned to the girl and nudged her back into the safety of the inner room that served as the library and followed after her.

"Did you like being ten?"

Talk about a loaded question. Carissa sunk into a soft-as-butter white leather chair and crossed her legs. "I suppose there were good days and bad days."

Olivia nodded as if she understood. For her sake, Carissa hoped she was only being polite.

Roger, Olivia's grandfather, meandered into the room. "I have a surprise for my princess."

Olivia's gaze shot up to her grandfather. "What?" Excitement bubbled in her voice.

"A friend of mine owns some horses. How would you like to go horseback riding?"

Carissa stifled a groan. Although she knew she couldn't keep her client under lock and key, horseback riding out in the open left too many variables for proper security especially in light of the mystery van. "Roger, could I have a word?" She stood and walked through the house until she reached the doors leading to the terrace, opened them, and went outside. No way did she want Olivia to hear this conversation.

He closed the door behind them. "What's going on? You look disturbed."

"Concerned is more like it. We had an incident while you were out. A white van approached the gate and sat there for several minutes. When my associate approached, the driver quickly drove away. We're concerned that the people who threatened your son and daughter-in-law may have located Olivia."

He frowned. "So soon? She's only been here a short time."

"We don't know anything for certain, but whoever was in that van did not want to be identified."

"Thanks for the update. I trust you and your team have everything under control."

"As long as she's in this house, she's safe. We're monitoring the property 24/7, and one of us is always with her, but once she leaves here, it complicates things."

He sighed. "I see. In other words, you don't want her to go horseback riding?"

"No, sir."

Roger crossed his arms and set his jaw. "Olivia can't live like a prisoner. I'm sorry, but she's going, and that's final." He pulled out his wallet and handed her a business card with the address of where the horses were boarded. "The property has miles of private trails for riding. I won't be taking her until Sunday after church. That should give your team enough time to get security measures in place."

"Sir, we aren't the secret service. We can't just go into any place we choose and take over." Carissa rested a hand at her waist. "But I have an idea."

"I'm listening."

"I'd like to ride with her."

He rubbed his chin. "I suppose that would work. I'd planned to ride with her myself, but I'm sure there's another horse we could borrow. I'll look into it and let you know."

"Thank you." She strode back to the library. Olivia sat with her legs tucked beneath her with her nose in the book.

Roger was right. The girl couldn't stay cooped up in the house all the time. Riding would be good for her, and security was doable. Plus, they had one thing on their side—no one would know to expect them. She'd make sure Roger kept their visit quiet.

Marc focused on the monitors. He couldn't get the van out of his mind. If only he had been able to get a better look at the driver and passenger. Frank's snores broke the silence.

Marc sighed and rubbed his eyes then stood and stretched. Carissa's espresso machine tempted him in spite of not being a coffee drinker. Serving in Afghanistan prepared him for the long hours, but not for Carissa. One minute he thought she'd accepted him as an equal, the next she treated him like a rookie. It was a bit confusing. But what bothered him most was his attraction to her. He'd finally found a job he liked, and all he ever thought about besides keeping Olivia safe was Carissa. A text on his smart phone drew his attention. Jack. His shoulders tensed. A text from his little brother couldn't be good.

5

Sunday morning, Carissa sat in the window seat of her bedroom at the Drummonds' with earbuds in her ears, listening to Julie chat about her latest date. She missed the girl-talk they'd once shared and didn't mind her friend's apparent success in the love department—at least one of them was dating.

"The new guy you're working with sounds hot. What's his story?"

Carissa gripped the phone tight. Why had she told Julie about him? "He's former military"

"Single?"

"Yes." Carissa winced. They'd butted heads over guys in the past. Julie was obviously interested in spite of her recent date that had been so wonderful. Unfortunately, they were attracted to the same type—tall, dark and handsome. However, Carissa required more than good looks, and Marc definitely had more going for him. The man was smart and quick-thinking, not to mention sweet. Good grief, she felt like an infatuated teen.

"We really need to get together and catch up in person," Julie dragged her back to the present. "I know you're on a case but you can't possibly expect yourself to work every hour of the day. When's a good time for you?"

"Julie, I'm sorry, but things are crazy right now. Getting away isn't possible. I'm going horseback riding later today with my client, and who knows what tomorrow holds."

"Where are you riding? Can I come?"

Carissa hesitated. What did it matter if Julie knew where they were going? She trusted her longtime friend, except where Marc was concerned, but she couldn't keep her from Marc forever. They were bound to meet sooner or later. "I need to check with Frank before I answer. If he gives the okay, I'll text the address."

"Are you serious? You have to ask if it's okay for me to join you somewhere? That's ridiculous."

Carissa winced at her friend's outburst. "Please understand this isn't personal. It's business. I would expect the same from Frank if the situation was reversed."

"Okay. I get it. I'll be watching for your text."

Carissa ended the call then shot off a text to Frank about Julie joining the outing. Thirty minutes later, her phone rang. "Frank. It's about time you called."

"I needed to do a quick check on Julie. She looks safe. If you think having her there is a good idea, then I'm onboard."

"Thanks, Frank. I need to try and make up for neglecting her. This will help a lot."

"I will never understand women." He disconnected the call.

She chuckled and shot off a text to Julie.

Meet us at that place east of town. We rode there a couple of times in middle school.

She stared at her phone waiting for Julie's reply.

I know the owners. Meet you at the stable. They have several horses and won't mind if I ride, too.

Carissa bit down on her bottom lip. Would she be endangering Julie? What if something happened while they were riding? Julie's martial arts lessons crossed her mind. She could hold her own in almost any situation.

She shot off another text. *Remember, I'll be working.*

Her phone rang.

"Hey, Julie," she answered.

"It's so much easier to talk. I hope you don't mind."

"It's fine."

"Thanks. Have you ever guarded someone around the clock like you're doing now?"

"Yes, but never for an entire summer. The longest has only been a week. I look forward to the summer's end so I can regroup and take a few days for myself."

"On the bright side, you're gainfully employed for the entire summer. When should I meet you?"

Carissa gave her the time then said good-bye and disconnected the call. She hadn't missed the comment about a job. Poor Julie had been let go from her job as a chef and had yet to find work. Maybe she could help her friend with that. Linda mentioned needing a caterer.

Marc's stomach growled. Definitely past time for lunch, but that could wait. He stood beside Carissa, who faced the ocean. Wet sand sucked around his tennis shoes. Olivia ran from the waves screaming and giggling at the same time. Although he was watching the child, he kept his attention on the people meandering nearby, too.

"She's so funny. I wish Linda or Roger could see this." Carissa grinned up at him. "You should join her. It'd do you good to have a little fun."

Marc frowned. "Me? I thought we were working."

"You'd still be working, just having fun, too."

"I don't think so. It's a little hard to stay alert while frolicking in the surf." Besides, he didn't play. He looked down at her and noticed the pucker in her brow. He nudged her shoulder with the side of his arm. "What gives? You're acting strange."

She shrugged. "I don't know. Guess I was hoping for a good laugh." She smirked and nudged him back.

Was Carissa flirting with him? "Hmm. Seems to me someone wants to get wet."

Her eyes widened, and she took a step away. "Don't even think about it, Marc. I'm armed, and I don't want my Glock ruined."

Marc sobered. "Bummer. Would've been fun." He winked and refocused his attention. What had just happened here? It almost felt like they'd crossed some invisible boundary and moved beyond co-workers for a moment. The idea brought a smile to his face.

"What are you grinning about?"

He tried to wipe the look from his face and only succeeded in grinning wider.

She nudged him again with her shoulder. "Come on. What gives?"

"I can't say. It wouldn't be professional."

Carissa's eyes went blank for a second. Then she caught her breath, and her cheeks pinked. "We should head inside. I don't want Olivia to get sunburned." She waved to the girl and Olivia ran toward them.

"What?"

"We need to go in."

"Can't we stay just a little longer?"

Carissa sighed. "Five minutes."

Olivia took off for the water again.

"Did I say something to upset you?" Marc hated to shorten Olivia's playtime just because he'd made Carissa uncomfortable.

"No. You reminded me that we have a job to do, which we can't do if we're…having fun." She pressed her lips together.

He didn't believe her, but whatever. There'd be other opportunities to get to know Carissa. He just hoped he didn't have to wait too long.

Olivia smiled at Carissa from atop the roan mare. "I saw a pretty white cat in the barn. She's going to have kittens soon. Can we come back and see them after they're born?"

"We'll see."

Olivia frowned. "But I want to see them. I love kittens."

"I didn't say no." Carissa held back a sigh. Why couldn't Olivia simply be content to be riding rather than demand something more?

"Okay." A smile replaced her frown. "I can't believe we're doing this. I've never ridden a real horse."

Carissa chuckled and glanced at Julie who snickered.

Marc stood beside Carissa and her mare. "Then what kind have you ridden?"

"Ponies. They're smaller. But I've only been riding twice."

"Ah, I see. Well the concept is the same." Carissa pointed to the helmet resting in Olivia's lap. "Shouldn't you be wearing that?"

"Grandpa told me to, but I didn't like the way it felt on my head."

Carissa patted the helmet she wore. If it weren't for Olivia, she may have forgone the nuisance, but setting a good example was important. Plus, the stable owner had insisted. "I'd like you to put the helmet back on."

"No!"

"Excuse me?"

"I don't want to." Olivia dug her heels into the side of the mare, and it bolted.

"Pull back on the reins!" Carissa knew her limits, and chasing after the girl wasn't an option. She glanced to Julie who looked as helpless as she felt.

"Get off!" Marc commanded.

She slid down, and Marc mounted the horse. "Tell her grandfather what happened. I'm going after her."

Carissa held her breath for a moment as Marc leaned over the front of the horse and raced away. She prayed the Lord would protect them both.

Roger hustled out of the barn leading a third horse. "What's going on? Where's Olivia, and where's your mount?" He looked down the trail where dust was beginning to settle.

"Marc went after her. She made the mare bolt when she dug her heels in too hard."

"I never should've let her out of my sight." Roger's face paled, and his breathing shallowed.

"It could've happened regardless of who was with her." She gentled her voice. "Marc rode like an expert. If anyone can help her, it's him."

"There's something to be thankful for. I'm going after them." Roger mounted the horse, clicked his tongue, and the horse moved forward.

"Wait!" Carissa did not want to be left behind. Olivia was her responsibility. "I'd like to come along. Is there another horse I can ride?"

"We can both ride mine." Julie held out her hand.

Carissa stuck her foot in the stirrup then mounted behind her friend about as gracefully as an elephant.

Finally situated correctly, Carissa wrapped her arms around Julie's waist. "Let's go."

Marc's pulse kept time with the beat of the horse's hooves. He and his mount moved as one over the dusty trail. He rounded a bend and spotted Olivia bouncing up and down atop the trotting horse. She wobbled to one side then righted herself.

Olivia slid to the side again. A scream ripped through the air, as she tumbled off the mare and into some bushes.

Marc slowed his mount and stopped beside the child. "Olivia!" He swung a leg over and dismounted.

With eyes closed, she lay motionless on the ground. He pushed the bush aside, leaned over her, and put his ear next to her face. Good, she was breathing. "Olivia, wake up." He gently patted her cheek. "Come on."

Her eyes fluttered, and she pulled in a deep breath. "What happened?"

"You fell off. How do you feel? Anything hurt?"

"I don't think so." She moved to get up.

"Hold on." He rested his hand on her shoulder. "Just relax for a few minutes."

She wiggled her arms and feet. "I'm okay, Marc."

Marc looked her over from head to toe. Aside from a few scratches, everything looked good and from what he could tell, nothing was broken. "Can you get up on your own?" If she could stand unassisted, she was probably fine, but just the same, he stayed close.

She sat up. "Whoa." Her head dipped.

"What's wrong?" He reached out his hand.

"I was dizzy for a second."

"Are you okay now?"

"I think so." Her brows puckered and her lips pulled down in a frown. Using her hands, she pushed up and stood. "Marc?"

"Hmm?"

"How are we getting back?" She asked in a small voice.

What happened to the confident ten-year-old he'd grown accustomed to? Was she really okay? "I figured we'd ride." The two mares munched at the grass along the trail.

"No way." Her dark hair swung from side to side. "That animal is crazy."

Marc pushed back the bush so she could get onto the trail. "How about you ride with me? What do you say?"

"I don't know." She looked up and down the trail. "Where's CJ?"

"She's probably right where I left her and having a fit because I took her horse."

Olivia's eyes widened. "Why'd you do that?"

He reached for the reins of Olivia's mount and then for his. "CJ isn't much of a horsewoman. Didn't you see the way she mounted? Don't even get me going about the way she sat." He stepped into the saddle, reached down for Olivia, and swung her up behind him. "Just relax and hang on." He patted the hand that gripped his shirt. "I won't let you fall." He meant it too. His heart about stopped when her horse bolted. She could've been seriously hurt.

Marc guided his mount alongside the other horse.

Olivia wobbled and slid to one side. He reached back and steadied her.

"Hey! You said you wouldn't let me fall."

"You're still on." He made a clicking noise and gently squeezed the mare's sides.

He looked around to make sure no one lurked nearby. Except for the chirping birds and breeze rustling through the tall fir trees, all was quiet. Satisfied they were alone, he turned and headed the way they'd come. About halfway back, they met up with Carissa, Roger, and Julie.

"Grandpa!" Olivia waved.

Roger looked as though he'd aged a few years. "Young lady, you nearly scared me to death. What happened?"

"I don't know. I guess I was too rough on the horse, and she went crazy. Then she stopped running and starting bouncing me like a pogo stick. I fell off into the bushes."

"Are you hurt?" Concern etched Roger's eyes. "Where's your helmet?"

"I only have a few little scrapes on my arms."

"What about the helmet? Did it come off when you fell?"

Olivia's shoulders slumped. "I didn't wear it."

"But I told you—"

"Excuse me, sir." Marc said. Roger's face had reddened, and Marc didn't want to risk putting the girl through any more trauma. "I saw the helmet near where Olivia fell and forgot to grab it. Would you take Olivia while I go get it?"

Roger blinked and focused on him. "Not necessary. I'll pay my friend for the helmet. Thanks for taking care of Olivia." He looked to his granddaughter. "Will you be okay while I'm gone?"

"Sure. CJ and Marc are fun."

"Thanks, kiddo." Marc patted her hand at his waist. "I don't get to ride like that very often. I forgot how much I like feeling the wind in my face." It'd been a long time since he'd ridden one of the two horses he and his three siblings shared in their younger years. Life had been good until their parents had been killed in an auto accident and he'd been separated from his brothers. Then everything changed. The thought of his family and the text his brother had sent put him back on edge. But he couldn't deal with that right now.

Olivia giggled. "Not me. Wind in your face while on top a large animal is highly overrated, but I'm glad you had fun." She laughed again. "Actually, it wasn't that bad until I fell off."

Carissa's eyes were filled with questions, but she kept silent. Julie turned their horse around, and they meandered back to the barn.

Olivia chatted the whole way. Clearly the event hadn't traumatized her too much, but from the firm set of Carissa's jaw and her narrowed eyes, he'd say his boss had a different view of the experience.

Later that same evening after Olivia was tucked in bed, Carissa tiptoed outside. Earlier, she'd asked Frank to hang out in the main house for a while so she could talk with Marc. Frank stood beside the door and entered as she exited. "Thanks. I'll text you when I'm ready to switch spots."

"Take your time. This is a welcome break from the monitors."

Carissa nodded and zipped up her windbreaker to ward off the cool breeze. She meandered to the cliff overlooking the ocean. The sun had set, and a red glow painted the horizon. If only she could go down and walk in the sand, but she planned to get a good night's sleep and still needed to talk with Marc. Turning from the view, she hustled to the guesthouse and entered without knocking. She found Marc watching the monitors. "Hey there."

Marc lifted a hand. "What's going on?"

"I wanted to thank you for this afternoon."

"No problem. You looked pretty upset about the whole thing. Are you okay now?"

"I was upset and frustrated at the situation, but I'm fine. Thanks for asking. I have one question though. How'd you know I'm not much of a rider? You took over like an expert."

He chuckled. "Olivia asked me a similar question. You didn't look comfortable in the saddle. I've been around horses quite a bit. I actually grew up on a farm. We had quarter horses."

"I didn't know that."

"Which part?"

Carissa chuckled. "All of it." She pulled up a chair beside him. "Frank said you were his foster brother."

"I was."

Asking what happened for him to end up in foster care was on the tip of her tongue, but she decided against it. "What was it like living on a farm?"

"A lot of work, but mostly enjoyable. We had chickens, turkeys, cows, and horses. We grew most of our own food. Our garden was huge. I hated weeding that thing. My mom needed an entire pantry for all the food she canned."

"Must've been nice to have siblings. I'm an only child."

"Really? I would never have guessed." A teasing glint lit his eyes.

She playfully shoved him in the shoulder. "What's that supposed to mean?"

Marc grinned. "You're independent, serious most of the time, and you seem to like being the boss."

"There's nothing wrong with any of that." She crossed her arms and kept her focus on the monitors, hoping he didn't notice that his observation unnerved her. He was absolutely right, and that bothered her more than she liked. She generally didn't allow people to get close enough to come to correct conclusions about her. But Marc was different.

"True. I'm sure being an only child must have its perks."

"Such as?" She hadn't minded being an only child, but she was curious how Marc would answer.

"Never having to share your new toys or never having to wear hand-me-downs or never having to fight with your siblings for your parents' attention."

"True, but I'd think having siblings would be fun. There would always be someone to play with."

"There is that." He eyed her as if trying to read her mind, or maybe he was trying to figure out if he could trust her. "Let's just say family complicates things. The bigger question is, what's eating you?"

"Who said anything is?"

"Me. You rarely come out here, and you've been off balance ever since the incident with Olivia."

"I have not." She pushed out of the chair.

He grasped her hand. "Hey. Don't leave angry."

61

Carissa looked pointedly at their hands. She couldn't think straight when he touched her.

He released his hold. "Sorry."

Her face softened. "I like you, Marc, and I see why Frank hired you. You're observant, and you read people well. I came over here to say good job today." She turned and left. Maybe she'd take that walk on the beach after all. Gravel crunched underfoot as she meandered through the garden toward the cliff. The stairs were only a few feet away when footsteps sounded behind her. She whirled around. *Marc.* Why had he left the monitors?

Carissa stopped. "What's going on?"

He spoke close to her ear. "I spotted a shadow along the east fence line."

Her focus darted toward the front door. "Olivia." She ran for the house.

6

Carissa burst through the front door and stopped short.

Frank sat in a chair to the right of the door. He stood. "What's wrong?"

"Shh." She kept her voice to a whisper. "Marc spotted a shadow along the front fence line."

His mouth stretched into a straight line. "He's sure?"

"I assume so."

Frank sighed. "I'll go check it out. It was probably someone passing by. But just the same, it looks like no one will get much sleep tonight."

"We can sleep later. Go." She gently pushed him toward the door. Hopefully, Frank was right, and it was nothing. If there was an intruder, she'd love to be in on the action, but her place was with Olivia. Chewing her bottom lip, she debated on whether she should enter Olivia's bedroom. She'd hate to accidently wake the girl, but on the other hand, there was a window in the room, and Carissa couldn't risk someone getting inside.

Carissa rushed up the stairs to Olivia's bedroom then gently turned the doorknob and poked her head inside. Olivia rested peacefully on her canopy bed, breathing softly. Tiptoeing to the window, Carissa avoided stepping on multiple items scattered on the floor. Satisfied the lock on the window was secure, she looked around the room once more and checked the closet before leaving. Just to be safe, she'd leave the door ajar.

Marc panned a flashlight back and forth along the grounds. His Glock was locked and loaded. So far, he hadn't seen or heard anything, and he'd covered two-thirds of the property. Where had the person gone?

A twig snapped.

He whirled to the right, raised his weapon, and cut the light, realizing he was a beached whale if the intruder wanted to take him out. "Don't move!"

"It's me. Frank."

The moon came out from behind a cloud and lit the space between them. Marc hustled to his boss. "It's quiet. No one's in sight."

"Good. I already searched the northern end of the property. The gate hasn't been tampered with, and there aren't any fresh tracks coming up from the stairs."

"How do you know? There's no way to differentiate one track from another."

"Every night just before sunset I rake a section of sand until it's smooth. If anyone comes up from the beach, we'll know."

Marc raised a brow. "Nice." Too bad he hadn't thought of that himself. Frank was an encyclopedia of information and good ideas. Taking this job was the smartest move Marc had made in a long time.

Frank patted him on the shoulder. "Let's go view the monitors. I'll back up the footage, and we'll take a look at what you saw. Maybe something will show up."

Still on alert, Marc walked with Frank to the guesthouse. "You don't seem overly concerned."

Frank opened the door and stepped inside the house. "With the location of the moon and it being so bright tonight, it would've been easy to create a shadow when someone passed by the fence."

"But wouldn't I have seen someone?"

"Maybe." They went into the observation room, and Frank replayed the last thirty minutes.

Marc kept his focus on the rest of the monitors. Shadow or not, there could still be a threat waiting to get to Olivia.

"Got it." Frank peered closely at the screen. "Just what I suspected. Look here."

Marc pulled his attention to the recorded image.

"See how the shadow falls. The head is on the inside closest to the house, and the shadows of the feet are closest to the fence. The person wasn't inside the property. Based on the build, I suspect it's a man just walking by."

"But why can't we see him?"

"Good question. Maybe he's wearing black."

"In the summer?"

"Why not?" Frank replayed the video once more. "He could be just far enough away from the camera that we can't see him."

The only place the surveillance covered beyond the property line was the gate. In all likelihood Frank was right. "Sorry for the false alarm."

"Don't worry about it, Marc. This has happened a couple of times to me, too. There's a learning curve." Frank pushed back and stood. "I'll go relieve CJ. She could use a good night's sleep." He chuckled. "Ten-year-old girls wear on my partner more than a ten-hour shift with the police department." He shook his head. "Go figure. Stay alert and text me if anything looks odd. No need to bother CJ, though."

"Got it."

"And don't sweat this. I'd take a false alarm over the real deal any day. See you in the morning."

Marc waved and gulped down the soda he'd abandoned earlier. When the adrenaline wore off, he'd need the caffeine to stay alert. Too bad they didn't have a fourth person on the job. It'd help ease the sleep deprivation.

Marc's thoughts drifted back to the conversation he'd had with Carissa about family. Sooner or later, he'd need to respond to his brother's text. Jack knew he often dropped below the radar, but his patience would only last so long.

Marc loved his younger brother, but Jack had a way of getting under his skin. He shook off the thoughts and refocused. Olivia's safety depended on him staying sharp, and that's what he intended to do.

Frank's update shot waves of relief through Carissa. Now she could get some sleep. She rubbed her burning eyes courtesy of a full day in the sun and very little sleep the night before.

After readying for bed, Carissa dropped between the soft sheets, pulled her quilt to her chin and smiled, thankful she'd thought to bring her treasured wishing blanket. Her mom had given it to her, explaining the blanket held special powers. All the person sleeping under it had to do was think happy thoughts, and everything would be okay. If only it really did have special powers, she'd wish for a quiet night filled with dreams of Marc. But she now knew God controlled the universe, not a wishing quilt.

Her mind drifted to work. Frank had been right to hire Marc. Sure, he lacked experience, but he brought a lot to the team, false alarm or not. He was paying attention, and that's what they paid him to do. She wanted to get to know their newest member better. Grinning, she closed her eyes as an idea percolated.

Her cell phone vibrated on the bedside table. She reached over and grabbed it. "Carissa speaking."

"Hey," Julie said. "I wanted to touch base with you, and see how the kid's doing?"

"Olivia's fine. I'm sure she'll be begging to go riding again soon."

Julie laughed. "Good for her. So what's the deal? Since when do you protect children?"

"She's the first, but I can't talk about it." With all the technology out there, one never knew who could be listening in.

"I understand. I also called to tell you I finally found a job. It's only part time, but anything will help."

Carissa scooted down and nestled the phone beside her ear. "That's great. Where are you going to work now?"

"A new little hole in the wall. They're only open for breakfast and lunch."

Carissa shot up. "That's great. I'm glad you found something."

"Thanks. I still have my eyes open for full-time work, but this will do for now."

"You should open your own place."

"That takes money, which I'm presently out of."

"I'll keep my ears open. Maybe Linda can hook you up with a catering job."

"That'd be cool, especially if it's an evening or weekend gig. Let me know. I see why you didn't want to tell me about Marc. He's amazing. That man can ride. You did say he's single, right?"

Carissa's heart thumped hard. She'd noticed Julie's

interest in Marc when they were riding and hoped she'd imagined it, but clearly, there was something there. "He's…uh…not your type."

"What's that suppose to mean? He seemed perfect to me."

"Let's talk about something else." Carissa did not want to get into another argument about a guy. Julie's love life was doing just fine without Marc.

"Oh, I get it. You want him for yourself."

She wanted to shout yes but held back. It would only make Julie more interested in him. "Whatever. I need to get some shut-eye. Catch you later." Carissa said good-bye and put the phone back on the nightstand. She'd meant what she'd said about Marc not being Julie's type. There was more to Marc than met the eye, and Julie would never take the time to look at the real man. There was no use arguing with her friend once her mind was set. It was best to drop it.

Things had been a little off between them for some time now, though neither of them would admit it out loud. She frowned. It seemed odd that Julie would be pushing so hard to renew their friendship, but she was glad nonetheless. She'd missed the late-night talks and fun times they'd once shared.

7

Carissa opened the trunk to her car.

Olivia darted out the front door and ran to her. "What took you so long?"

"Sorry, I visited a friend while I was out." She finally made good on her promise to have coffee with Julie. Their time together had gone too fast though. She'd have to make a point of inviting her over sometime. They'd gotten along great, and Carissa was excited that things felt right between them again.

"You have other friends in Lincoln City? I thought you only knew my grandparents."

Carissa bit her bottom lip. She'd have to be more careful. Olivia was smart. "I do have other friends. You remember my friend Julie, don't you? She went riding with us."

"Kind of. I didn't realize you knew her before that day. I thought you'd just met. Why aren't you staying at her place for the summer?"

"Because I was invited here, and I'm your nanny for

the summer. Remember?" Didn't the girl remember being shot at in Arizona? Had she blocked it from her mind? "I'm also here to make sure you stay safe."

"Oh yeah." Olivia shrugged. "What'd you buy?"

"Food. I have everything planned for tonight. You and your grandparents are going to roast hotdogs on the beach and then make s'mores. We'll all watch the sunset and maybe tell a few stories." She reached in, grabbed the cloth grocery bag, and closed the trunk. "What do you think?"

Olivia stayed by her side. "Sounds yummy. What about Marc? Will he be there, too?"

Carissa pretended to think about the idea. She'd hoped the child would request Marc's presence. It was part of her master plan to get to know him on a personal level. "I think that could be arranged."

Olivia smirked.

"What are you up to?" Carissa liked her client, but she'd discovered the girl had a mischievous streak.

Olivia looped her arms behind her back and twisted gently from side to side. "Nothing." Her voice belied her response. It was definitely more than nothing.

Carissa opened the door to the main house. The scent of fresh baked cookies drew her further into the home. "I'm back."

"In the kitchen," Linda called.

"Mmm. Your grandma's been busy." Carissa brought the bag into the kitchen and spotted a cooling tray on the granite countertop. "The cookies look and smell delicious."

Linda turned. She held a spoonful of dough. "Help yourself, Carissa. Let me know what you think."

"Can I have one, too, Grandma?"

"Of course, dear. I thought I'd pack these up for our picnic dinner."

"Yum." Carissa brushed crumbs from her fingers. "They're as good as they look. May I take a few to Frank and Marc?"

"My goodness. I always forget about those two. There are paper plates in the cupboard at your feet. Take them a dozen. We'll have plenty."

Carissa reached down for a paper plate then put the hotdogs away and set the graham crackers, chocolate bars, and marshmallows on the counter. "I thought we could make s'mores tonight. I didn't realize you'd be baking."

Linda twisted her mouth then waved the spoon in the air. "I can put these in the freezer for another time."

Olivia squeezed her grandmother around the waist. "Thanks. I can't wait to make s'mores. My friends at home find sticks and cut the ends into points for roasting the marshmallows."

Linda gave her granddaughter a side hug. "Sounds like fun, but I don't know about the sticks. We have some skewers made for roasting over an open fire."

Carissa shrugged. "Works for me."

"Olivia, how about you go up to your room," Linda said. "I'd like to have a word with Carissa."

Olivia snagged two more cookies and zipped from the room.

"What's up?" Carissa asked.

Linda lowered her voice. "I understand there was some commotion last night. Is everything okay now? I mean is it safe for Olivia to be on the beach tonight?"

Carissa pulled out a bar stool and sat, resting her forearms on the counter. "Marc and I'll both be there, and Frank will monitor your property. I'll do my best to keep Olivia from harm."

"I know you will. I want to apologize for my attitude. I sincerely didn't realize the seriousness of the situation when you first arrived. I spoke with my son earlier today, and he told me about the house being shot at the day you brought Olivia here. I'm so glad she's with us and not there. My son would be devastated if anything happened to his little girl. Of course, we all would be, but he'd blame himself." She opened the oven, removed a pan, then replaced it with another. "To be completely honest, I was against having strangers in my home. I thought it'd be too intrusive, but you and the men have fit right in. Olivia thinks the world of you. I don't know how she'll handle not having your company when she goes home."

"Thank you. Hearing you say that means a lot." It was nice to see the woman soften. "I appreciate your honesty. I know it was hard for you at first, but guarding Olivia is our pleasure. She's a fun kid, and I'm sure she has tons of friends to hang out with at home."

Linda nodded. "Speaking of Olivia, I suppose you should be off doing your thing."

"Now that you mention it, yes. I'll run these over to the guys first though." Carissa quickly placed a dozen cookies on the plate, covered it with plastic wrap, and went outside with an extra spring in her step. Although she'd sensed a shift in attitude from Linda, it felt good to hear the words.

Marc sat on a sand chair across the open fire from Carissa with Olivia to her right. Roger and Linda sat to his sides. They each held a hot dog on a long metal skewer over the flames. A breeze kicked up, creating a chill, but the fire warmed them.

"Marc, tell us about growing up on a farm." Carissa zipped up her windbreaker and tucked a hand inside the sleeve.

Marc sucked in his breath and wished she'd stop asking him about his family. Sure, she'd asked about the farm, but it was a family farm and an unwelcome subject.

Olivia sat up straight. "You lived on a farm? With like, goats and chickens and pigs?"

The excitement in her voice made him smile. Regardless of how he wanted to avoid this topic, he couldn't deny this girl. "No goats, but we did have chickens, a couple pigs, cows, and horses. We also had land with fruit and nut trees, and our own vineyard, and the biggest summer garden ever." He crossed his ankles and leaned back. "My mom said every year after hours of canning in the hot kitchen with me and my brothers and sister, she'd cut back the next year, but that never happened."

"Wow. My mom barely cooks." Olivia pulled her hotdog from the fire and groaned. "It's burned."

Carissa pulled her own away and blew on it. "Looks just like mine. I'd say they're perfect."

Olivia looked doubtful but wrapped a bun around it anyway. "Where's the mustard?"

Linda assisted her, and conversation died as everyone ate. Marc admired Carissa's seeming ease, but he knew her senses were on alert for trouble as much as his. At least their job was made easier by the lack of people out tonight.

After eating, Olivia loaded her skewer with a marshmallow and held it low over the fire. "Am I doing it right?"

Linda nodded and placed a couple squares of chocolate on a graham cracker. "When it starts to turn brown, bring it here, and I'll slide it between the crackers."

Olivia pulled the puffy delight from the fire. "How's this?"

"Perfect. Bring it here." Linda squished the marshmallow between the crackers and handed it to her granddaughter.

Marc almost laughed at the delight in the girl's eyes. Either she really loved s'mores or she'd never tried one before, but either way, her excitement was fun to see.

Olivia bit into the treat, and her eyes widened. "This is so good!" She said with a full mouth. "Can I make another one when I'm finished?"

Roger chuckled. "Sure, kiddo. Just don't make yourself sick. Your daddy used to gorge himself on those things when he was a kid."

"He never makes them anymore." Olivia's shoulders slumped.

After another round of s'mores, the girl jumped up. "I'm bored. Can we go for a walk down by the water?"

Linda shook her head. "I'm not dressed for getting wet. Maybe Carissa and Marc will go with you."

Marc pushed up. "Sounds good to me. You game, Carissa?"

"Sure."

He offered her a hand and pulled.

"Thanks."

The threesome meandered close to the ocean with Olivia in the middle.

Olivia took each of their hands. "Are you two a couple?"

"You seriously need a hobby," Carissa said.

"I have one."

"Really? Do tell." Carissa swung their entwined hands.

"I read."

Marc chuckled. "Reading a gossip magazine doesn't count."

"I read books, too." Indignation filled the child's voice.

"Sure you do." Marc ruffled her hair.

"Give the kid a break, Marc. I've seen her read books. In fact, I'd like to borrow the one with the horse in it."

"Any time. But neither of you answered my question." She dropped their hands and faced them. "Do you like each other?"

"Of course we do." Marc tapped her nose. This kid needed to back off before she made things awkward.

"No." She giggled. "I mean like boyfriend and girlfriend."

Too late. He glanced over at Carissa, who dipped her chin and fidgeted with the zipper on her windbreaker. "CJ and I are friends. We're not a couple."

Knuckles pushed into his shoulders. "What was that for?"

"I told you not to call me that," Carissa said

"What?"

"CJ."

"Olivia gets to and so does Frank. It's only fair."

"Yeah. Come on, CJ," Olivia pleaded.

Carissa glared at Marc and shrugged. "Okay, fine."

He widened is eyes. "Really?"

Olivia smiled, winked at Marc, then ran toward the water.

He caught his breath. The kid was ten going on twenty. He chanced a look at Carissa.

Her attention focused on someone up the beach. "Have you noticed that guy's been keeping the same distance from us since we've been walking? It's like he's pacing us, but I don't know how, since his back is to us."

"You suspect trouble?"

"I'm probably being paranoid. It seems weird, though, especially since we've stopped so many times. Olivia!" She waved her arms overhead.

Olivia waved back.

Two joggers closed in on Olivia, and Marc's pulse raced. Carissa's suggestion that the man ahead was up to no good put him on edge. He ran toward Olivia and got to her just before the joggers continued by without even a glance toward them.

Olivia propped a hand on her side. "What's wrong, Marc?"

"Nothing."

"Then why'd you leave CJ all alone? I think she likes you. My best friend at home has a boyfriend, and she says he's dense about relationship things. Are you dense, Marc?"

"Your best friend has a boyfriend? How old is she?"

"She's twelve."

That explained so much. "CJ is my friend. Of course, she likes me." He walked along beside her.

Olivia sighed. "I mean like, like you." She bent down and picked up a broken sand dollar.

Marc struggled to keep a straight face. Water rushed toward them. "Watch out." He grabbed Olivia's hand

and ran. The earth shifted beneath him. Releasing Olivia's hand, he tucked into a roll.

Olivia giggled and offered him help up.

"Thanks." He brushed off the sand and glanced toward Carissa who was grinning and clapping. He bowed.

"I want to be alone. Go walk with CJ." With both hands on his back, Olivia shoved him in Carissa's direction.

"Pushy. Pushy. Just watch out for sneaker waves."

"I will."

Carissa shot him a heart-stopping smile. A tingle zipped up his spine. He was in trouble.

8

Laughter bubbled up in Carissa. The man sure knew how to fall. If the bodyguard thing didn't work out, he'd probably make a good stunt double. He certainly had the finesse and good looks to do the job.

Marc jogged up beside her. "Tumbling is my claim to fame."

"I noticed." Her mouth stretched into a smile. "What're you doing? I thought Olivia wanted your attention."

He rubbed the back of his neck and looked everywhere but at her. "She wants to be alone."

"Figures." They strolled arm in arm, following Olivia as she kicked at the water.

"So you grew up on a farm, have lots of siblings, and you served in the Army. What else should I know?"

He pursed his lips for a moment. "I don't know. I've been doing odd jobs since I left the service."

"You're searching for something," she murmured.

Olivia moved further away from the ocean, plopped

down and dug her toes into the sand.

"What about you? What makes Carissa Jones tick?" Marc asked.

"Not much to tell. I was a cop. Now I'm a bodyguard."

His gaze grabbed hers and held. "I know there's more behind those pretty green eyes than the job. But if you insist on only talking shop, why'd you leave the police force?"

"Frank had an itch to go into business for himself. I didn't love being a cop. He proposed his idea to start Protection Inc., and I jumped at it."

"What made you want to become a cop in the first place?"

The man had a way about him that made her want to talk. Not something she usually did willingly. She took a deep breath and let it out in a whoosh. "My mom was mugged when I was ten. I was there. It changed me." She looked over at him and read the surprise and sadness in his eyes.

"Wow. What happened?"

"We were in Portland for a day of shopping. I wanted to eat dinner at this really cool place downtown, so we took the MAX train from Clackamas Town Center." She closed her eyes at the images, still so vivid. "The man ran off once he had what he wanted, and we called the police. Mom talked with them forever."

"Harsh. Did you ever get to go to the restaurant?"

"No. I didn't want to eat after having a gun pointed

at my head"

Marc stopped and looked at her. "I thought he mugged your mom."

"He did. By threatening to shoot me. She wouldn't give up her purse at first so he turned his gun on me."

"That's—"

"I know. Let's talk about something else." She crossed her arms. She'd never told that story to anyone, including Frank. Her parents didn't talk about it either. Somehow the time she'd orchestrated to get to know Marc turned into a confession session of her own.

"But I have another question."

"Not until you answer one for me."

He dipped his chin.

"Do you have a wife, girlfriend, or fiancée?"

"Nope. You?"

"No wife or fiancée, but I have a few girlfriends." She smirked.

He leaned in and butted his shoulder against hers. "Funny. So no boyfriend or anyone special in your life?"

"Most men are not attracted to someone in my line of work. I think they find it intimidating."

"Not me."

Good to know. Even in the dimming light, Carissa saw the embarrassment on his face. Looked like he'd said more than he meant to. "It's getting dark." She tucked her hands into her windbreaker's pockets. "And cold. We should get Olivia and head in." She observed Linda and Roger smothering the fire and packing up their belongings a little bit ago. They'd headed up the stairs hand in hand. The couple could be stuffy, but their love for each other was clear.

The whirring of a helicopter grabbed her attention. It approached from the south and didn't look like the coast guard. Maybe it was a scenic charter, but it was too dark to know for certain. "We need to get Olivia inside." She motioned for the girl to come to them and, thankfully, she hopped up and ran full speed.

As Olivia sped by, she shouted, "Race you."

The chopper was probably nothing to be concerned about, but Carissa wasn't willing to take any chances. She raced after Olivia staying at the girl's heels.

Marc swept Olivia up and tossed her over his shoulder. Though winded, Carissa did her best to keep up, but Marc pulled away. She looked up as the chopper flew overhead and on past the estate. Relief coursed through her. The copter appeared to have no interest in their client. She ran up the stairs and for the main house.

Carissa charged through the front door of the main house and spied Marc and Olivia, sitting on the couch in the library with smirks on their faces.

"We beat you," Olivia announced.

"You two cheated."

Marc raised his hands. "I won fair and square. But you're right, she cheated." He pointed to Olivia.

"No I didn't. You're the one who tossed me over your shoulder."

Marc chuckled. "Nah. You hijacked that ride."

Carissa laughed. She definitely needed to have fun more often. "I'm going to sit on the deck. Olivia, how about you get ready for bed while Marc and I look at the stars?"

Olivia's face lit into a wide smile. "Okay." She stood and trotted upstairs.

"Smooth." Marc stretched and rubbed his back.

"What's the matter, old man? Can't carry a seventy-pound girl up the stairs without hurting yourself?"

He made a face and followed her out the sliding glass doors. "The helicopter's gone."

"Let's sit and see if it passes back." She grabbed the binoculars by the door. "If it does, I'll be ready."

"Carissa?"

"Hmm?" She kept her gaze on the sky over the water.

"Is the mugging the reason you became a cop and then a bodyguard?"

Her gaze slammed into his, and the sound of the crashing surf faded. "Yes."

"You want to save the world from the bad guys?"

"One person at a time." And with Olivia it felt personal. Maybe because the girl was the same age she'd been when the mugging occurred. She cleared her throat. "Look. The chopper's coming back." Carissa pushed the binoculars to her eyes and sighed. "It's too dark. I can't get a visual on the N-number."

"Let me try." Marc held his hand out. "You're right.

Do you think it's trouble?"

"Probably not, but we can't be too careful. It's been quiet since Olivia arrived. I expected something to happen by now."

"It's only been a few weeks. Maybe the threat hasn't tracked her down yet."

"Perhaps." A niggling in her stomach said otherwise. These people were desperate to stop or apprehend the technology Olivia's parents possessed, and she suspected they were desperate enough to follow the child across the country to make their point. She pushed up from the chair. "I'm going to bed."

Carissa approached the kitchen and heard more than one familiar voice. She stepped into the gracious space and spotted Julie sitting at the counter with a cookie in her hand laughing at something Linda had said. "Hi, there. This is a surprise." She'd invited her friend to stop by sometime but thought she'd at least call first.

Julie swiveled in the seat and motioned to the chair next to her. "Frank let me in. This place is locked down like a prison."

Carissa narrowed her eyes, trying to get her friend to hush.

"Personally, I don't know how you—" Julie rambled on.

"Come on up to my room, and we'll talk." Carissa looped her arm through Julie's.

Julie allowed herself to be dragged from the kitchen but not before thanking Linda for the cookie.

Once in her bedroom, Carissa closed the door and dropped her voice. "What was that all about?"

Julie's face fell. "What do you mean?"

"The prison comment."

"Oh. I was only making conversation." Julie had the grace to look apologetic. "I didn't mean to say something I shouldn't. I'm sorry." The woman had a habit of speaking without thinking.

"Forgiven," Carissa said. "What brought you by?"

"You told me to stop in sometime, remember? Plus, you mentioned that Linda might have a catering job for me."

"Might." She plopped onto the edge of the bed and motioned Julie to the corner chair. "But showing up here and being friendly won't get you a job. You should cook for her."

"You're right. I didn't think of that." Julie bit her bottom lip and stood. "Is Linda more mac and cheese or smoked salmon frittata?"

"Definitely the salmon, but Olivia would love the mac and cheese."

"Hmm. Maybe I'll do both." She swung open the door. "Thanks, Carissa. See you soon. I'll let myself out." She strode down the stairs and out the door.

Carissa frowned, unsure how she felt about having Julie entrench herself with this family. She shook off the thought. Julie was only looking for work, and Linda might hold the key to a lucrative future.

Marc studied the monitors for trouble. Camera one focused on the entrance gate where nothing moved. No shadow, nothing. He switched his gaze to camera two aimed at the closed front door to the main house. A creak behind him alerted him to another presence.

"That you, Frank?"

"Yeah." He walked into the room and sat in the empty chair. "How'd it go tonight?"

"Fine. No problems."

"I meant with CJ. She give you any trouble?"

"Only when I called her CJ. But I'm making progress. I now have permission to call her by her nickname." He chuckled. "Funny thing is, I'd rather call her Carissa."

Frank leaned back and rested his foot on his knee. "Sounds about right. What do you think of her?"

Marc glanced at his boss and shrugged. "What's with all the questions?"

"Nothing. Thought I saw something between the two of you."

He shifted in his seat. "Guess you need glasses." What was it with Olivia and Frank? There was nothing between him and Carissa other than a working relationship. Sure, at one time, it'd felt like there could be something growing between them, but now... The idea warmed him from the inside out. He really liked her, and if they weren't on this case 24/7, he'd ask her out, but things were complicated.

Frank stood. "I'll be in the main house until morning. Call if you see anything."

"Will do."

"And, Marc?"

"Hmm?"

"I have 20/20 vision." Frank left the room.

A few minutes later, Marc spotted Frank on the monitor as he opened the front door and went into the main house. Marc twisted the cap off a soda and took a long drink. His body craved sleep, but instead he fed it caffeine. Too bad the original schedule hadn't worked out. Sooner or later he'd adjust to staying awake all night and only getting four to five hours of sleep during the day since someone always had to be on the monitors. In the meantime, he depended on sugar and caffeine to keep him alert.

Although he watched the monitors with care, he couldn't help thinking about Carissa and what it must have been like to be ten with a gun pointed at her head. He shivered. He'd served in Afghanistan, and even he'd never come face to face with the enemy's weapon. He admired her for taking the high road and making something of herself rather than wallowing in fear and self-pity.

Not only that, she'd clearly risen above the incident. The twinkle in her eyes and zeal for her job were evidence enough. How did someone move past an experience like that and become a better person for it? Someday, he'd have to ask her.

A horn honked over and over. A quick glance at monitor number four showed that Frank's SUV alarm had been tripped. The headlights flashed on and off. Movement on camera two drew his attention. Frank walked outside with his gun drawn. Marc continued to watch the monitors, but maybe Frank would need backup. No, this could be a trick used to distract him from his post. He stayed glued to the surveillance cameras. If someone was out there besides Frank, he'd find him.

9

Carissa woke with a start. She blinked rapidly to clear the fuzz from her eyes. A horn honked over and over, dragging her from beneath the covers. Flipping on the bedside lamp, she slipped on a pair of jeans, tugged a sweatshirt over her head, then grabbed her Glock and made sure it was locked and loaded. Ever so slowly, she twisted the doorknob to her bedroom and peered down the hall one way then the other—*clear.*

She opened Olivia's door. A lump bulged in the middle of the bed. It appeared to be Olivia, but she tiptoed closer to confirm.

"CJ?"

She tucked the weapon behind her. "Yes, it's me. Sorry to wake you. I just wanted to make sure you were okay."

The horn stopped.

"Was I talking in my sleep?" she mumbled then rolled over and closed her eyes.

Carissa wished she could fall asleep so easily. She

checked the locks on the windows then looked under the bed and in the closet before leaving the room.

Once she trotted down the stairs, she peered out the window, facing the front. Frank sat inside his SUV. The horn honked again, and the headlights flashed. Looked like another false alarm. Carissa padded up the stairs and into her bedroom.

Her mind ran through the events of the day and ended with the horn episode. She processed the security check once more, making sure she hadn't missed anything. Then, she finally rested back on the bed and pulled her quilt up to her chin. Yawning, she closed her eyes, and her body melted into the mattress. Maybe sleep would come after all.

Marc chased her through the surf. Carissa tripped and landed on all fours. Smiling she tilted her head and spotted Marc to her left. He said something she couldn't hear. "What?"

Admiration shone in his eyes, and he offered a hand up. He pulled her to standing then stepped closer. "You are so beautiful." He slowly ran his fingers up her arm and cradled her head in his palms. He lowered his mouth to hers and—

"Rise and shine, sleepy head!"

Carissa's eyes shot open. "Olivia," she groaned. "You interrupted the best dream." She rolled over and covered her face with the extra pillow.

Olivia hopped onto the end of the bed. "Tell me about it."

Carissa tossed the pillow at the girl. "No."

"Please." She let the word drag out in a whiny voice. "I never remember my dreams."

Carissa scooted up to sitting and drew her knees to her chest. "Sorry, but some dreams are private."

Olivia giggled. "Was it an embarrassing dream? Sometimes my friend Samantha has dreams she refuses to talk about. She's older than me and has a boyfriend. I think they're about him, and that's why she won't tell me."

Warmth crept into Carissa's face. She buried her head against her knees. No way would she tell a ten-year-old about that dream. Not that it was bad, but it was embarrassing. "How about you go make your bed? I'll take a quick shower. Then we can go see what your grandma has planned for the day. Maybe we can go to Regatta Park."

"What's that?"

"It's this really cool park along Devil's Lake. It has a large climbing structure and other fun stuff. Plus, I'm sure there will be lots of other kids there to play with."

"I'm too old to play at a park." Olivia narrowed her eyes and gave her a haughty look. "How about the beach instead."

"Okay. I thought you might enjoy doing something different." She waved her away. "Scoot. I need to take a shower and get dressed."

Olivia hesitated. "This quilt is pretty. Is it yours? Grandma doesn't have anything like it."

"Yes. My mom gave it to me when I was about your age. It's a wishing ring pattern, but I call it my wishing quilt. I take it with me whenever I travel. It helps me sleep better."

Olivia frowned. "I wish I had a blanket to help me sleep."

Carissa frowned. The girl slept like a log. "I suppose it's hard to be away from home for such a long time."

"Yeah. I miss my mom. How does the blanket work?"

"What do you mean?"

"You said it helps you to sleep. How?"

"My mom gave it to me at a pretty crazy time in my life, and it reminds me of being safe and snug in my bed at home, which helps me relax and fall asleep."

"Cool." She hopped off the bed and closed the door on her way out.

Carissa's heart hurt for all the girl was going through, but she breathed a little easier now that Olivia had left the room along with her probing questions. Good thing she didn't want to go to the park—security would have been a nightmare. That suggestion popped out thanks to her fuzzy, dream-laden brain as a desperate attempt to change the subject.

Marc looked out the living room window and squinted against the late afternoon sunshine. Carissa held the hose and sprayed suds off her car while Olivia stood in the path of the overspray, clearly trying to get wet. He chuckled and let the blind fall back into place.

"Sleep well?" Frank asked as he poured a cup of coffee then sat at the table.

Marc shrugged and strode to the kitchen. "I don't know how you drink that stuff." He pulled a soda from the fridge and twisted the lid off. Leaning against the counter he took a long draw from the bottle.

"I don't know how you can stomach soda first thing in the morning."

"It's four in the afternoon."

"So? We both woke up a short while ago. Feels like morning to my stomach." Frank sipped his coffee and sighed. "Nothing like a strong cup of coffee to start the day." He opened his Bible and focused on the print.

Marc settled onto the sofa and considered the information Carissa revealed about herself last night. He had the impression she didn't share her story with many people. He glanced over at Frank, who remained deep into his reading. What drew a man to read the Bible so religiously?

Ten minutes later, Frank joined him on the sofa holding a second mug of coffee. "How're things going?"

"Depends."

"On what?"

"What you're talking about." His brother's text still bothered him. Maybe Frank would have some insight. "You know I have a large family."

Frank nodded. "Yeah. One of the reasons I like you. Makes you a team player."

Interesting observation, although he wasn't sure he agreed. "My brother is getting on my case. He wants to know where I am."

Frank rubbed his chin. "And you want to tell him. I assume you can trust your brother."

"Of course, but after my slip to the hotel clerk about my destination, I wasn't sure it would be allowed."

Frank took a swallow of coffee and set the mug on the coffee table. "Go ahead and fill in your brother. I don't see the harm."

Marc frowned. He'd kind of hoped Frank would tell him no. He hated how nosey his siblings were. Then again, maybe Jack wanted something else. As soon as Marc had a chance, he'd send an update to his family.

"I get the feeling you have more on your mind."

Should he mention what Carissa had told him? Frank had to already know. "CJ told me about the night her mom was mugged. You sure this job is healthy for her, considering?"

Frank rubbed his chin. "You lost me."

"It seems to me that with Olivia being the same age Carissa was when it happened and the fact that she thinks she needs to save the world, this particular job might cause her to take unnecessary risks."

Frank rubbed his chin between his fingers. "I have no idea what you're talking about. Maybe you better start from the beginning."

Marc frowned. "I thought you knew. Carissa's going to have my head if I tell you."

"Not if I take it off first. Spill."

Marc sighed and told Frank everything.

"That sure explains a lot."

"You really didn't know?"

Frank stood. "Think I need to have a talk with my partner. Give me a few minutes."

Marc watched from the window as Frank approached Carissa. His shoulders tensed. If she wanted Frank to know, *she* would've told him. Boy had he messed up.

Carissa knew that walk. Frank wanted something, and it wasn't good. She looked around for an escape and took a few quick steps toward the stairs leading to the beach.

"CJ," Frank's voice had an edge. "Don't even think about it."

She sighed and waited for him.

"I'm going inside, CJ." Olivia skipped toward the house.

Too bad she couldn't retreat with the girl. But whatever was up with Frank needed to be dealt with. She crossed her arms. "What's up?"

"Walk with me." Frank headed toward the guesthouse then stopped and turned to face her. "You've been my partner for eight years and not once did you mention you and your mom were mugged. You don't think that's something I ought to know?"

Carissa shrank back and swallowed the lump in her throat. *Marc.* "No I don't. It never affected me on the job. I was a good cop, and I'm a good bodyguard."

Frank's face softened. "CJ, don't you see your judgment could be clouded where Olivia is concerned? If I'd known about your past, I never would've taken on this job." He raised his hands. "What would you do if someone put a gun to your head again?"

"That's not fair."

He sighed. "Did you at least get counseling? Haven't you ever heard of post-traumatic stress?"

"Of course," she snapped. "Have I done one thing to endanger our client? No. Olivia is safe and will stay that way." She set her jaw and jutted her chin.

"I wasn't talking about Olivia." His voice softened. "I was thinking about you. And you never answered my question. Did you get counseling?"

"No." She crossed her arms. "I'm fine. You're overreacting. Now if you don't mind, I'd like to find Olivia and see what she's up to."

"I do mind. The girl is safe. You don't have to spend every waking minute with her. The house is secure." He raked his hands through his hair and took a deep breath. He let it out slowly and shook his head. "Aw, CJ. I'm sorry. When Marc asked me if I thought this job was healthy for you, I didn't know what he was talking about and pushed him for more information. To be honest, I didn't give him a choice. When I found out I didn't know you like I thought I did, I lost it. I'm sorry I overreacted, but I think of you as the daughter I never had."

"Forgiven," Carissa said softly. Frank's explanation

made sense, but Marc had no excuse whether Frank forced it out of him or not. He never should have brought it up. Period. "Are we done here?"

"Almost. What's going on with you and Marc? He's known you a few weeks, and you tell him your deepest, darkest secret."

Clearly, trusting a confidence to Marc had been a mistake, one she wouldn't make again. "He doesn't know me better than you do." She perched on a stone garden bench. "I'm not sure what's going on with us." She took a calming breath. "We were talking the other night, and it popped out. I'm comfortable with him. It's funny, too, because when I first met him, I was uneasy. Guess that goes to show first impressions aren't always right." She frowned. "Although, he can't keep his mouth shut."

"In all fairness, I pulled it out of him."

"He didn't have to say anything in the first place."

"What's done is done. I see a lot of potential in Marc. And for the record, he only brought it up because he was concerned for you."

Carissa nodded and stood. Frank's endorsement meant a lot. But she was still a little miffed at Marc. "Would you mind keeping an eye on things for me? I'd like to speak with Marc privately."

"You-hoo." Linda waved from the front steps of the house.

Carissa and Frank exchanged a look. This was the first time Linda had sought them out like this. Curiosity drove Carissa toward her. "Can we help you, Linda?"

"I was hoping you would all join us for dinner tonight. Your friend Julie is cooking, and it sounds wonderful. I'm considering hiring her to cater the silent auction at the museum in the fall."

"Julie's a fabulous cook."

"We'll find out tonight." Linda turned to Frank. "I know you have equipment to monitor, but maybe just for this evening you could get away. Julie wants everyone there."

Frank rubbed the back of his neck. "That would leave the estate vulnerable to intruders if someone isn't watching the monitors. I don't think so. I'm sorry, Linda, but I must decline. Marc and CJ could join you."

Linda waved her hand. "I figured as much. But I had to try." She looked to CJ. "I'll expect you and Marc at six. Does that work for you?"

"Yes, I'll let Marc know." Carissa had eaten with them every night, but Marc had never been invited.

"Wonderful! I'll see you later." She turned and went inside.

Frank stroked the whiskers on his chin. "Julie's been poking around a lot lately."

"I thought you liked her."

"That's not the issue. She's here too much."

"What am I supposed to do, Frank? She's my friend and wants to hang out. I can't exactly leave and spend a girl's night out with her. Having her here is much easier."

"I get it. You have a life. Marc's having a similar problem with his family. If I had a life, I suppose I'd be having the same issue." He said dryly. "Is there anything I need to know?"

"She was out of work for a while after the restaurant she worked at was sold and the new owner brought in his own chef. Her current job is only part time, and she's trying to find full-time work. The catering gig was my idea. I thought it'd be a nice supplemental income."

"I see. Let me know how dinner goes." He grinned. "Bring me a plate?"

"Sure."

"Oh, and I'd like to know if we'll be graced with Julie's presence on a regular basis."

"We should be done here well before the catered event, but I'll keep you in the loop." She eyed her partner. "Stop worrying, Frank. You'll give yourself an ulcer."

10

"I can understand why you're angry, Carissa." Marc patted the seat next to him and divided his attention between CJ and the monitors. "Really, I do. I didn't mean to betray a confidence. I assumed—"

"Exactly!" She towered over him.

He glanced up at her. "Hold on a minute. I figured if you told me, then Frank would know." It had to mean something that she'd told him and not Frank. Was there more going on here than he realized?

Carissa sighed and sat beside him. "Frank was pretty miffed." Her voice softened. "I'd never told anyone until you."

He stilled and searched her face for answers. "Why didn't you say so? And why tell *me*?"

She shrugged. "Guess I figured with your time in Afghanistan you'd understand." She stood. "I shouldn't have said anything. Let's just forget it." She took a step.

He reached out and grasped her hand. "Hold on a sec. I appreciate that you trusted me. For the record,

I'm sorry about bringing it up to Frank, and I'll keep my mouth shut in the future."

She grinned. "You'd better. Of course, that's assuming there is a next time."

He released her hand. "I hope so." His voice matched her reflective tone.

"Oh, I forgot to tell you. We're invited to dinner in the main house at six. Julie's cooking. Don't be late." She exited quietly from the room. He focused on the monitors and spotted her walking across the garden that divided the two homes.

"CJ, hold up." Frank strode toward her. "I received intel regarding the threat against Olivia."

Carissa altered her course and headed toward the backside of the property facing the ocean. "What do we know?"

"You want the good or bad news first."

"Good."

"My source confirmed a plan to kidnap Olivia and hold her for ransom."

If that was the good news, she sure didn't want to hear the bad. Carissa stared out over the ocean as seagulls sailed into the wind elevating their wings in an arc. "Are we talking money, or do they want the technology?"

"Unknown, but we should be prepared for

anything. No matter what, we can't allow them to get to Olivia."

"That goes without saying." So far nothing he'd told her warranted the serious look on his face. She'd surmised most of it already, especially after the attack at the girl's home. "What aren't you telling me?"

Frank scowled. "They have Olivia's mother."

Her heart tripped. "When? How?" Olivia would be devastated.

"I don't know any details, but when Olivia went off grid, it appears their focus shifted to the mother."

She looked off in the distance then snapped her focus back to Frank. "You said they still plan to try and grab Olivia. If they have her mom, what's the point?"

"Insurance?" Frank shrugged.

Carissa worried her bottom lip as her shoulders tightened. "Is Dr. Drummond going to give in to their demands?"

"The FBI is on the case."

At least they had that to be thankful for. "Once they apprehend the people responsible, this will all be over. Do you think we should move Olivia in case we're missing something?"

"I spoke with her grandfather, and he refused. They still don't want Olivia to know what's going on."

"She already knows her dad was threatened. We couldn't exactly hide the fact that we were being shot at."

"I understand, but she's not to know about her mother. I'd rather not spoil this summer for her if I can avoid it."

"Her mother was abducted! How are they going to hide that?" This job was never easy, but the game had changed.

"Apparently, she only speaks with her parents once a week, and they called last night. They have a week to find her before the next phone call."

"I guess she's not as close to them as I thought." She couldn't imagine a little girl only talking to her mom once a week.

"Her parents work a lot."

Carissa rubbed her forehead. "Okay. So what now?" Her brain felt like a jumbled mess at this turn of events. "I think we should ask again about moving her. I'm not comfortable with this arrangement."

"You're welcome to try, but keep an open mind, CJ. They are her grandparents, and they only want what's best for her."

"Then I'll have to convince them that moving her is best." Carissa strode toward the house and stepped inside.

A pan dropped in the kitchen, and Linda let out a cry. Carissa ran into the room and spotted the older woman with hands planted on the counter top and her head down.

"Are you okay, Linda?"

She wiped her eyes before looking up. "I've been better. I suppose you heard."

"Where's Olivia?"

"Listening to music in her room." Linda moved to

a bar stool and sat leaning her elbows on the granite countertop. "We've always been proud of Sean. He's brilliant, and his work will save so many lives. I don't understand why anyone would want to stop that."

Carissa thought about what Olivia's mom must be going through right now. She shook the horrible image away. She couldn't go there. It hit too close to home. Her mom had only been mugged, but that moment had changed everything.

Maybe Roger had the right idea keeping Olivia out of the loop and blissfully unaware that anything was wrong. Moving her would only create questions. And with those questions, came answers no ten-year-old girl should have to hear.

"If you'd like to call Julie and cancel dinner, we'd understand. I could pick up a couple of pizzas. The guys and I could eat in the guesthouse and give you and your family some privacy."

Linda looked up with red eyes. "No. I need to make a decision soon about a caterer, and Julie will be here any minute. Besides, Olivia is looking forward to having Marc with us." She attempted a weak smile. "She's quite the matchmaker."

"I've noticed." Carissa crossed her arms. "I'll go check on her. Don't worry. We'll do everything possible to keep her safe."

"I know you will. Right now I'm most concerned for my daughter-in-law. I need to pray." Linda closed her eyes, and her lips moved.

Carissa left the room quietly and headed up the

stairs. She may have only known the Lord for a short time, but His impact on her was astounding—she should have thought to pray for Olivia's mom also. She shot up a quick prayer for the woman's safety and release.

Music blared from the other side of Olivia's door. She tapped the door then pushed it open. "Hey, kiddo. What are you up to?

Olivia lowered the music volume. "Playing a game." She held her smartphone and her eyes followed the movement on the small screen.

"Okay." Carissa backed out of the room and went downstairs. The house was secure, so she made her way over to the guesthouse. Without knocking, she walked in and found the men in the observation room. "Did Frank fill you in on the latest, Marc?"

He nodded with a scowl. "You make any progress with the grandparents?"

"No. I didn't try. I changed my mind. Roger is right. We can keep Olivia safe here, and she'll never have to know about her mother. Unless the unthinkable happens."

"Let's not go there," Frank said. "There's nothing we can do except pray the FBI is able to find Olivia's mom and that we keep our client safe. We're good, but divine help is always appreciated."

Carissa closed her eyes and followed Frank's lead.

Marc looked from CJ to Frank and bowed his head.

"Amen," Frank said.

Marc lifted his head and locked eyes with CJ. He motioned toward the door. He stood and waited for her to accompany him to the next room.

A smile crossed her face. "I noticed Julie arrived with dinner. Are you ready to head over?"

"Sure. Let's go." Frank took over his post, and they went outside. "Is the weather in Lincoln City always so pleasant?"

Carissa chuckled. "No."

He grasped her hand in his and detoured to the cliff overlooking the ocean. "I'm glad we aren't moving Olivia. I'd miss this view." He'd taken her hand, but she made no comment.

"Yeah, I'll miss it when this job is finished." She smiled. "Come on. I don't want to keep them waiting." She pulled from his grasp and walked toward the main house. "Can I ask you a personal question? Not as your employer, but as a friend."

"Sure."

"Are you a Christian?"

"Wow. That came out of nowhere. Why do you ask?" Not that he minded having this conversation, but it was unexpected.

"Just wondering. I saw you praying earlier, but I had the impression that faith in the Lord might not be a part of your life."

Now her question made sense. "I am a Christian,

but I'm uncomfortable talking about my faith. As far as praying goes, I pray, but I've always figured I should only bother Him with the big stuff."

"Mrs. Drummond's abduction isn't big enough?" Surprise filled her voice.

"Not what I meant. Life and death is big. I think what I'm getting at is, because I only think to pray about the big things, I forget to pray."

She nodded. "I get that. I tend to try and deal with things on my own and forget to ask for help. That being said, I know He cares about the little things, too."

"How can you be so sure?"

"There's a chapter in the book of Matthew that says God knows the number of hairs on our head. It seems to me that if He knows something as insignificant as that, He must care about every aspect of our lives."

Marc nodded. He remembered the verse but hadn't thought about it that way. What she said made sense, but still, he didn't like bothering God with little things.

"I feel like you're not convinced."

He shrugged. "I'm chewing on the idea."

"Fair enough, but keep this in mind. He loves us a lot—the kind of love that doesn't stop when we mess up. A God like that must care about the little things to my way of thinking."

He nodded and stopped at the front porch to the house. "Remember how I said I'm not comfortable talking about my faith?"

She nodded. "Too much?"

"Maybe, but this was the first time that I can recall not minding all that much."

Carissa grinned and lifted her chin slightly. "Remember. We have to pretend everything is normal."

11

Sitting on a bench in the garden between the two houses, Carissa gazed up at the stars. Crickets chirped and a gentle breeze rustled the trees. Strategically placed lights lit the landscape in a soft glow. Dinner had gone well. Linda raved over Julie's meal, and Olivia hadn't seemed to notice the tension the adults tried to hide. Marc had been charming, and Julie had soaked up his praise of her meal. Aside from Julie's obvious interest in Marc, the evening had been a success.

Footsteps crunched on the gravel walkway. "I heard dinner was a hit for your friend," Frank said.

"Mm-hmm. Marc's on watch?"

"Yep." Frank eased down beside her. "Care to share what's on your mind?"

"I've got nothing."

"Can't fool me. I know you too well. Saw you on the monitor. You're chewing on something. If you're worried about Olivia, stop. We'll keep her safe."

She shook her head. "That's not it. I know we'll do our best." Although Olivia's mother's abduction raised her concern for the girl.

Frank blew air between his lips in a slow puff. "Then what is it?"

Other than the surf below, the evening was quiet. In her head, she knew pursuing a relationship with Marc would be tricky. There was the whole boss-employee thing to consider not to mention what a distraction he was. "I really like Marc, and I don't know what, or if, I should do anything about it."

"Ah. Now I understand. I had a feeling about the two of you. I can't tell you what to do, but be careful. I don't want Olivia's security compromised because your mind is elsewhere."

Carissa pushed up. "Understood. I think I'll take a walk on the beach." She sure wished Frank had thought about that before introducing Marc into her life, especially since he had seemed to be trying to play matchmaker.

"Rake the sand before you come back."

She nodded and ambled away. The sun set over the horizon as she took the first step down. Red and pink colored the sky. She continued down the steps and slipped off her shoes, checking the bulge in the sole before moving on. Cool sand seeped between her toes as she meandered toward the water. The briny smell of the ocean tickled her nose.

At least down here, there weren't eyes watching her

every move. The cameras on the estate were necessary for security but lacked the privacy she desired. Frank's words played over in her head. She couldn't let Marc distract her. They had a job to do and nothing else mattered.

A wave crashed, and water surged toward her. She turned and ran. Water nipped at her heels. The hem of her jeans now wet, dragged in the sand. Okay, maybe thinking about Marc was a distraction, and it needed to stop right now.

Marc noted the slump in Frank's shoulders as he walked into the main house—odd. Unease settled in his gut. Carissa hadn't looked happy when she'd walked away either. What had he missed? Had something happened to Olivia's mother at the hands of her kidnappers and no one told him? No. They wouldn't keep quiet about that.

At least everything on the monitors appeared normal. He didn't know how people who watched monitors for a living survived. Talk about tedious. Carissa was lucky she never worked the observation room. Then again, she spent most of her time on the front line with Olivia.

Speaking of CJ, she popped into the view of camera five at the beach access. Her shoulders slumped, too. What was going on? He crossed his arms and leaned back into the seat. Maybe she and Frank had a fight. That had to be it.

Instead of walking toward the main house, she headed toward the guest lodging. He sat up straight, now alert. A minute later, he heard the door latch.

"Hey, there." Carissa plopped onto the seat next to him.

"You and Frank have a disagreement?"

She whipped toward him, her eyes narrowed. "Why would you ask me that? You're supposed to be watching the monitors for intruders, not spying on your bosses."

He raised his hands. "No harm meant. I was only concerned. You both look like you lost your best friends. What's going on?"

"Nothing." She sighed and stood. "Think I'll head to bed and sleep off this rotten mood. I'm sorry for snapping. I know it's hard to ignore people on the screens. That job's got to be as tedious as finding a needle in a haystack."

"Not that I've ever tried, but yeah." He gently grasped Carissa's arm as she moved to pass him. "If you need someone to talk to, I'm a good listener."

She closed her mouth and hesitated. "Okay."

"Okay?" He couldn't believe she'd taken him up on his offer so readily. He reached for his soda.

"Yes." Carissa eased into the chair beside him. "You should know that Julie has a thing for you."

He nearly spewed the drink all over the monitors. "That's what you want to talk about?"

Carissa chuckled. "Guess that came as a surprise. Are you interested?"

"In Julie?" He glanced her way. "No."

"Whew. If you were, I was going to have to talk to Frank about letting you go as soon as this job's over." She winked and nudged him with her shoulder.

He drank in her playfulness and relaxed. Now this was the woman he'd grown to care for. Whoa, where'd that come from? "CJ?"

"Hmm."

"What would it matter if I was attracted to Julie?"

Her faced pinked, and she ducked her chin. "You know I don't like being called that."

Nice deflection. "You said it was okay."

"I suppose I did give you permission." She glared at him, but a smile tugged at her mouth.

"CJ is a term of endearment."

"Ha. Only Frank called me that until Olivia."

"And now me." He grinned.

She pressed her lips together in a half smile. "You just wait. I'm going to come up with a name for you, and you'll regret this CJ business."

"Doubtful," he said softly.

She cleared her throat and stood. "I should be going. 'Night, Marc." She strode away.

"'Night," he said to the empty room. He couldn't name it, but something had changed between them tonight. Something big.

Carissa passed Frank as she climbed the stairs. "Everything quiet?"

"Yep. Sleep well."

"I'll try." She tiptoed into Olivia's room. She'd gotten in the habit of looking in on the child. Olivia lay quietly on top of the covers. Carissa drew a blanket over the girl, closed the door, and went to her own room.

Her wishing ring quilt covered the top of the bed. She ran her hand over the quilt her mother had given her so long ago and remembered her mother's penned words like she'd opened the card only moments ago. But in reality she'd read the note so many times she'd memorized the message. *Your grandmother and I hand-stitched this quilt. She told me we are strong women and never falter when life gets tough. This quilt represents courage, but more than that, love. You see, every female in our family stitched a quilt as a sort of coming-of-age.*

I know you'd rather do about anything than sew, so I'd like to give you mine. The pattern is called the Wishing Ring. When you lay beneath it, you can wish upon the quilt, and your wish might come true. You'll never need to be afraid, and it will help you sleep. Carissa blinked rapidly. She'd never forget the love that went into making this quilt and would cherish it forever.

She changed into pajamas and slipped beneath the covers remembering many nights where, as a child, she'd wished for her dreams to come true. But she didn't believe in fairytales anymore and treasured the blanket for the sweet memory. Her eyes grew heavy and she gave in to the gentle wave of sleep.

A scream ripped through the silence. "Olivia!"

12

Carissa bolted from her room and nearly plowed into Frank. "Was that Olivia screaming?"

"Sounded like her to me." He drew his Glock.

Linda and Roger rushed down the hall in their bathrobes. "Is Olivia okay?" Linda asked. Her face pale against her silver hair that hung straight to her chin. She reached for the doorknob.

"Stop!" Frank whispered. "I need to make sure there's no threat.

"But she's not screaming anymore," Linda said.

"Grandma. CJ."

Carissa cut in front of Frank and opened the door with caution. Once she assessed the room was safe, she motioned for Linda to enter.

Linda flipped on the light, rushed into the room, then sat on Olivia's bed. "What's the matter, sweetie?"

"I had a bad dream. Can I sleep with you and Grandpa?"

Hesitation welled in Linda's eyes. "Well, I…"

"Would you like to borrow my wishing quilt?" Carissa clamped her mouth shut. She hadn't slept without that blanket since the day her mother had given it to her.

Olivia's eyes widened. "Really?" She scrunched her nose and studied Carissa for a few seconds. "How will you sleep without your blanket? You said it helps."

"I can manage one night. But you have to promise to be very careful with it. It's old and delicate."

"Promise." Olivia's eyes were huge and looked sincere.

Carissa turned and walked with purpose to her bedroom. She gently folded the quilt then carried it back to Olivia. Frank and Roger were no longer hanging out in the hall. Good. They didn't need to know she still slept with her childhood blanket.

Linda helped tuck the quilt up to Olivia's chin. "You want to tell me about your dream, Olivia?"

"No."

"It might help to talk about it," Carissa said.

"I'm okay now."

With a fleeting look at her quilt, Carissa said good night. She waited in the hall for Linda.

"Thanks for what you did in there." Linda closed the door softly. "Your quilt is beautiful."

"My mom gave it to me when I was a kid."

"You've taken very good care of it." Linda looked down the hall toward her own bedroom. "Guess I should try and get some sleep, too." She padded to her room and slipped from view.

Carissa ambled down the stairs.

Frank sat near the bottom. "Everything good with our girl?"

"Yes." She covered her mouth and yawned. "It's been a long day."

Frank held out his wrist and pointed to the time. "The day has barely begun. Try to sleep. We need you fresh and alert."

"I'm too wound up."

"I insist, CJ. Go back to bed."

"How am I supposed to sleep?"

"Count sheep." He deadpanned.

Carissa wrinkled her nose at him. Counting sheep never worked.

Marc tilted his head. "Rough night?"

Frank leaned against the doorjamb of the observation room. "Between Olivia screaming in her sleep, nearly scaring me to an early grave, and CJ, yes."

"What happened?"

"Olivia had a bad dream."

Marc stood and stretched. Carissa would be with the girl for the next eight hours, so it was time for some shuteye. "What happened with CJ?"

"Nothing really. But I could tell she was rattled."

Marc didn't like the answer, but what could he do? He moved down the hall.

"Hold up a sec." Frank followed him and stopped a couple feet away. "I know something is brewing between you and CJ, and I want you to know if you hurt her, you'll answer to me."

Marc blinked. Where did that come from? "Did she say something?"

"Sleep well." Frank turned to his own room and shut the door.

Marc stared at the closed door, tempted to knock and insist Frank fill him in on what he thought he knew, but common sense and self-preservation won out. Boss man clearly had no intention of sharing, but the warning had met its mark. Mess with Carissa and answer to Frank. No way did he want to go there, but if he had a chance with CJ, he wouldn't pass it up. The woman made his pulse race, and he sensed she felt the same way about him. Only time would tell.

"What do you mean she let you borrow her wishing blanket?" Marc was trying to understand what Olivia was rambling on about as she slipped off her sandals to walk along the beach. Somewhere between Olivia's bad dream and her wanting to sleep with her grandparents, he'd gotten lost.

Olivia picked up her flip-flops and meandered through the strewn driftwood littering the beach. "CJ's mom gave her a special quilt when she was a kid. It's called the Wishing Ring quilt, but she shortened it to the wishing blanket. It's supposed to make the wish of the person sleeping under it come true, but CJ said that's just a story." She looked up at him. "Can I go run in the surf?"

"Sure. I'll watch from here." Marc settled against a large log. He worked at hiding his shock. CJ slept with a security blanket? The visual image didn't match the strong, confident women he'd come to know. Then again, he had seen her vulnerable side the night she shared about the mugging.

"Hey there." Carissa came up to the giant driftwood he was leaning against and bumped shoulders with him. "What are the two of you doing?"

"We were going to walk, but Olivia wanted to play in the surf."

Olivia ran up to them and stopped. "We're going to go for a walk and see the tide pool. You want to come?"

"Love to." She looked at Olivia. "Your grandma asked me to remind you about dinner."

"What time is it now?"

"Four-thirty. Dinner's at five-thirty tonight."

"Will you let me know when it's time to head up? I don't want to make Grandma angry."

"Of course."

Marc reached for Carissa's hand. "Come on. If we're going to visit the tide pool, we'd better hurry."

Olivia ran ahead of them.

"I heard you had an interesting night."

Carissa yawned and nodded. "Yeah. Olivia had a nightmare."

"Any word on her mother?"

"No." A frown wrinkled her forehead.

Olivia stopped about twenty feet ahead of them. "Hurry up you guys!"

Marc scanned the area for anyone who looked suspicious. A man with a metal detector searched for buried treasure not far from Olivia, but he seemed disinterested in the girl. Several other people strolled along the shoreline, and a woman jogged in the wet sand with her dog. No one seemed to be a threat, but he knew any one of them could mean trouble. He gripped Carissa's hand tighter. "Come on. Let's catch up."

She pulled free from him and took off in a sprint. He dragged behind for a second, but he quickly got his footing and took the lead.

Olivia squatted at the tide pool and looked up at him. "You're weird."

"Where'd that come from?" Marc worked at not being insulted.

"That's what I thought, too, at first." Carissa squatted beside the girl. "But once you get to know him, he's kind of fun." She winked at him.

His heart melted a little. He was seriously falling for this woman. "If the two of you are going to talk about me like I'm not here, I'm leaving." He pretended to be put out and turned from them.

Olivia jumped up. "I'm sorry, Marc. You're not that

weird."

He chuckled. "Thanks, kid." His cell rang. It was Frank. His pulse picked up. Frank almost never called, and when he did, it usually wasn't good.

13

Carissa glanced in Marc's direction. Something about the look on his face had her on edge. Who called? She looked up and down the beach for any threats and relaxed a bit. Whatever it was, it didn't appear to have anything to do with Olivia.

He pocketed his phone. "I have to go." He leaned in close to her ear. "There's a problem with one of the cameras, and Frank needs me to check it out."

"Should I come too?"

"No. Stay here with Olivia until dinner. That should give me enough time to fix the issue without her noticing."

"What are you two whispering about?" Olivia moved close to them and stood on tiptoe, presumably in an effort to hear their conversation.

"Nothing that concerns you, Miss Nosey." Marc tapped her nose.

Carissa watched Marc hustle for the stairs leading up to the estate.

Olivia shielded her eyes with her hand and stared up at her. "What's wrong, CJ? You look worried."

"I always look like this when I'm hungry." Carissa pointed to a starfish to divert the girl's attention. "Look, Olivia."

The child shrugged and studied the starfish in the tide pool. "Cool."

Carissa's gaze swept up and down the beach and then to the ocean. No one would get to Olivia on her watch.

"CJ?"

"Hmm?"

"How come my grandma never spends time with me?"

"What do you mean? She reads with you, and we had that dinner on the beach, and you got pedicures together."

"I know." Olivia kicked at the sand. "But I came to spend the summer with her, and I spend almost all my time with you. I don't think she loves me."

"Oh, sweetie." Carissa's chest tightened. "Of course she does."

"Then why does she always send me off with you?"

Carissa looked out over the ocean. "I guess she figures you'll have more fun with me. I don't think your grandma is a sand castle kind of lady. She's more of a society person. You know, she likes art exhibits and symphony concerts."

"But she can still do those things. I like art and

music. And I'm a little sick of hanging out on the beach. Tide pools are only interesting so many times." Olivia plopped down on the sand, drew her knees to her chest, and buried her toes in the sand. "Do you think the people trying to stop my dad are still causing problems?"

"Why do you ask?"

"I want to go home. When I get back to the house, I'm going to call my mom and tell her."

Carissa caught her breath. Olivia couldn't call home right now. Not with her mother missing. She knelt and faced the girl. "I hope you'll reconsider. You've made my summer so much more fun than it would've been. I can't remember the last time I spent so much time down on the beach. Plus, my friend Julie could come over and give us some cooking lessons."

"I'd rather hang out with my friend Samantha. She likes to shop at the mall, and we make up stories about the people who walk past us."

"That sounds like fun. We could do that here on the beach."

Olivia hopped up. "No, thanks. I'm going to go call my mom. The danger has to be gone by now. I've been here forever."

Carissa's eyes widened. They hadn't fooled this girl for a minute. Granted, they'd had to fill her in after being shot at in Phoenix, but Olivia had been so cool about everything, Carissa had been certain she'd blocked it from her memory. This sudden change was not good. Carissa kept pace with the girl as they strode to the stairwell. "Maybe you should give yourself a day or two to think about this. I'd hate for your grandmother to get her feelings hurt."

Olivia stopped short and looked up at Carissa. "I hadn't thought of that, but..." she drew the word out. "I—I don't know."

Marc quickly found the problem with the camera and reconnected the loose wire. Strange, but there was a first time for everything. He found Frank in the observation room. "Do you have a clear picture now?"

"Yep. What was the problem?"

"Loose wire. Any word on Olivia's mother?"

Frank nodded. "I just got the call. She's in FBI custody. They found her out on the highway trying to stop traffic. The perpetrators must not be as good as we thought, because she escaped."

Marc's stomach knotted. "Please tell me they got them."

"I wish. And the woman was no help either."

"Was any information regarding Olivia compromised?"

"They're still looking into that."

"What else do we know?"

"Nothing." Frank nodded toward a monitor. "CJ's with Olivia. Go fill her in, and stay close to them."

"You got it." Marc turned to go. He caught up to Olivia and Carissa in the garden where they were feeding the Koi. Funny, he'd barely noticed the fishpond until now. He sidled up to Carissa and took her hand. "I have news."

She nodded. "I think the fish are full, Olivia. How about you go wash your hands for dinner? I'll be in shortly. And please think hard before you call your mom."

"Okay." She kicked at pebbles as he meandered toward the house.

Once the girl was a safe distance away, he told Carissa the news about the girl's mother. "What's this about calling her mom?"

Carissa rolled her eyes. "She wants to go home."

"No way."

"I know, but it's out of our hands if her parents allow her to return."

"That's it? We're supposed to just forget about her?"

"Yes. Don't get attached to the people you protect, Marc. We only take short-term jobs, and it doesn't pay to get emotionally involved."

"How do you do it?"

"Based on the hurt in my heart, not very well."

Marc's eyes widened. "I'm sorry. I didn't realize."

She shrugged, and her eyes glistened. "I don't want her to leave yet. Not until the threat is neutralized."

Marc opened his arms, and Carissa stepped into his embrace.

"Thanks. I needed a hug."

He spoke into her ear. "We can protect Olivia, and her parents know that. They won't let her go home."

"I hope you're right. I'd better get inside." She stepped back.

"Before you go…"

Carissa's gaze held him. How could a woman wield such power over him? He saw the same desire in her eyes that he felt and ran his fingers from her hairline down the side of her face, stopping at her jaw and tracing it with his thumb. It was now or never. He leaned toward her. His mouth inches from her full lips.

"I need to get inside." She stepped back and fled across the garden and into the house.

Disappointment shot through him. Clearly, Carissa felt something for him. Maybe he'd scared her, but that didn't seem likely. He looked toward the main house, debating whether to follow or not.

A text from Frank drew his attention. *Get in here.*

Marc drew in a deep breath and let it out slowly. He couldn't catch a break.

Another text. *NOW.*

It wasn't like Frank to shout. He two-timed it to the guesthouse and flung open the door. Frank would be in the observation room. He took a second to gather himself then went into the room. "What's so urgent?"

"What do you think you're doing?" Frank growled. "I told you not to mess with CJ."

"I'm not messing with her. I happen to care about—"

"She's off limits."

Marc crossed his arms and felt his neck heat. What was he missing? "Hold on a sec. CJ is a grown woman. You don't get to dictate who she does or doesn't spend time with." His eyes widened. "You have a thing for CJ."

"No. She's like a daughter. Don't mess with this papa bear, Marc. Foster brothers or not, you won't like the outcome."

Marc met the steel glint in Frank's eyes and swallowed the lump that had formed in his throat. "Understood. But you should know we have a connection. The kind that doesn't come around all that often."

"I hear you, but I'm asking you to back off, at least for now. I need CJ focused on Olivia, not on you."

Marc felt the slap as if it was physical and took a step back. "Are you saying this as my friend or my boss?"

"Both. If she's distracted, she may miss something, which could result in disaster. You don't want to be the cause of our failure. CJ would resent you."

Marc frowned at Frank's sensible words. "Okay. I'm going for a run before I take over here." He left the room and quickly changed into running gear. He may not like what Frank had to say, but he'd honor the man's request.

His cell buzzed and he pulled it from his pocket. *Jack.* "Hey there."

"It's about time you answered." Jack didn't sound angry, but relieved.

"Yeah. Sorry. I've been working non-stop and needed to get permission."

"To talk with your own brother? What kind of job are you doing anyway?"

"I'm a bodyguard."

Silence.

"Hello? You still there?"

"I'm here. Just surprised. You being careful?"

"Of course."

"It's good to hear your voice. Been too long."

He'd been in a bad place since rejoining the civilian world, and his siblings had all been worried about him. What his brother didn't understand was their concern pushed him further away. He needed to figure things out on his own. "Like I said, I've been busy. Everyone doing okay?"

He listened to his brother fill him in on all the family news and was surprised to find out he was going to be an uncle. His little sister was pregnant with her first. Funny, how life kept on going with or without him. "Tell everyone hi and not to worry. I'm fine."

"You got it. And thanks for answering." The line went silent.

Marc pocketed his phone, relieved to have that conversation over with. Now for that run.

Carissa chewed her bottom lip and leaned against the deck railing. The ocean crashed below, mimicking her thoughts. Unsettled didn't begin to describe how she felt. But it had little to do with Olivia, who slept upstairs.

Marc caused her discombobulation. She would've enjoyed his kiss, but she couldn't let herself go there. Not so long as he was her employee.

"Hi."

She turned toward the glass doors as Frank stepped onto the deck.

"Beautiful night." He leaned his back against the railing. "Everything okay?"

"Yes. Olivia's snug in her bed. Good news about her mom. I can't believe she escaped."

"Me, too. I thought for sure she'd be found dead."

Carissa frowned. "How long do you think we have before they locate Olivia?"

"Don't know." He turned and faced the ocean. "Something on your mind?"

"Plenty, but nothing I care to talk about."

He pushed away from the railing. "Fair enough. See you in the morning."

A shiver zipped through her. She couldn't shake the feeling something big was about to happen.

14

The sun shone bright in the early morning sky. Marc strolled the grounds doing his usual security check before heading to the guesthouse for some shuteye. It'd been a long quiet night, and his eyes burned from staring at the monitors. The cameras covered almost every inch of the property, but they couldn't be too cautious. Quiet had ruled the past week, but tensions were high. Olivia's parents had refused to allow her to return home, and the child had turned gloomy. So far, they'd managed to keep her tucked safely away from those intent on harming her.

A classic fire engine red pickup slowed on the street and pulled into the driveway at the gate. It couldn't be. Marc strode to the gate.

Kyle Richards, an old army buddy, sat behind the wheel. He killed the engine and got out, meeting Marc at the entrance. "Long time no see. How's it going?"

Marc's shoulder's tensed. "Hey, man. What're you doing here?" More importantly, how'd Kyle find him?

They'd been out of contact since he took this job.

"I was driving up the Oregon coast and remembered you'd mentioned taking a job in Lincoln City. Thought I'd try and find you."

Marc pressed the button for the automatic gate. "Come on in." He waited as Kyle drove his pickup onto the property and parked. He met him in the driveway in front of the main house.

Kyle turned off the engine and stepped out. "Looks like this job's treating you well." Kyle's gaze took in the estate and then settled on Marc. "You're moving up in the world."

A knot formed in Marc's gut. He'd served with Kyle, and they'd been tight, but something didn't feel right. "No offense, man, but you never said why you're here. Or how you found me."

Kyle's face sobered. "I was hoping to crash here for a few days and take in the sights."

"Marc!" Frank's sharp tone ripped through the morning air. He strode toward them. "This a friend of yours?"

Kyle held out his hand. "Marc and I go way back. I'm Kyle Richards. Nice to meet you."

"This is my boss, Frank Graham." And from the look on Frank's face he might not be his boss for much longer. Letting his buddy onto the property probably hadn't been Marc's smartest decision.

"Kyle is passing through." He moved toward Kyle's pickup, but the man held his ground.

"Actually, I hoped Marc could put me up for a few nights."

Frank frowned.

Feeling loyal to his buddy, he ignored the churning in his pit. "He's a good guy, Frank. We served together in Afghanistan. You can trust him."

Kyle looked from man to man and for the first time since he'd arrived, a flicker of uncertainty settled in his eyes.

"How 'bout you take your friend out for breakfast and give me a call later."

Marc understood that Frank was buying time to check out Kyle. That's the way the man operated—trust no one. Good. If he passed Frank's inspection, everything would be fine. At least Olivia hadn't come outside. Of course, it was barely eight o'clock, and the kid usually opened her eyes around eight thirty. Kyle had definitely chosen a good time to drop in.

"There's a great hole-in-the-wall cafe not far from here." Marc gave Kyle directions. "I'll meet you there."

"Sounds good." Kyle got behind the wheel of his pickup and drove out.

Frank rounded on Marc. "You know this job is sensitive. I'm disappointed in you. You had no business allowing Kyle onto the property or better yet, letting him know your location. Your brother was one thing, but this…" He spun on his heel and strode back to the guesthouse.

He followed sputtering, "I didn't tell him I was here. I don't know how he found me."

Frank stopped. "For real?"

"Well, I must've mentioned Lincoln City, but that's it. I promise. At the time, I didn't know me being here needed to be kept secret. It's not like I work for the CIA or something."

Frank narrowed his eyes. "Go meet your friend, and while you're gone, I'll check him out. If he passes, and if Linda and Roger don't mind, he can crash on the guesthouse couch for a couple nights. But keep him away from Olivia. Understood?"

"Yes, sir." He turned and left. Once on the road, he couldn't shake the feeling something wasn't right. Even if he'd shared what city he was living in, Kyle shouldn't have been able to narrow down the residence.

Traffic was light for a change, so he made good time. He parked then stepped inside the cafe. Kyle sat along the wall and lifted a hand when he spotted him.

Marc pulled out the chair at the two-person table and squeezed into the tight space. "Sorry it took me so long."

"No problem. Your boss is intense."

"He can be." He ignored the menu. "How'd you know where I was staying?"

"The last time I saw you, you mentioned the name of the hotel where you planned to stay. All I had to do was stop in and ask if they had any idea where you went after you checked out."

"But that was over a month ago. Someone actually remembered me?"

Kyle chuckled. "Guess you made an impression on the woman. She was cute but not your type."

He groaned, remembering exactly who Kyle spoke of. The woman had flirted non-stop and had been more than willing to give him directions. He hadn't seen her since.

"You've always had a way with the ladies."

His thoughts shifted to Carissa. He knew she cared for him, but she held him at arms' length. He didn't get it. He saw in her eyes the same longing he felt for her, but they couldn't get past whatever was causing her to keep her distance. At first, he'd assumed she was out of practice where men were concerned, but now he was beginning to think she had something against him. Kyle showing up certainly wouldn't help that.

The waitress took their orders and left.

"Your being here put me in some hot water with my boss."

"What? Are you under lock and key or something?"

"Something."

Kyle leaned forward. "I didn't mean to cause you trouble."

"It's okay." He leaned back in the chair and crossed his arms. "I'm still curious about what brought you to Oregon and why you looked me up."

Kyle's gaze darted around the tiny dining room then rested on him. "I received a call saying you're in trouble. You owe someone money, and he asked me to get it from you."

"That's nuts. Who sent you here?" He didn't owe anyone money. Had the people after Olivia figured out he was on her security detail and used his friend to get to him? It was a long shot, but he wouldn't put anything past them. He might be a rookie, but he knew better than to underestimate a desperate criminal.

Kyle looked around the small space again then leaned in and lowered his voice. "He offered me a ten percent cut if I persuade you to pay up." He waved a hand. "I don't care about the money. The guy set off all kinds of internal alarms, so I figured you needed someone to watch your back."

"You could have called." Marc's neck and his shoulder muscles tightened.

"You know I don't trust technology."

The ancient pickup his buddy drove easily dated back to before computers controlled cars.

"Any idea who I supposedly owe?" Unease crept up his spine. Was the man here right now watching, waiting to see where he would lead him? This time he looked at the patrons at the other tables. No one paid him any attention.

Kyle shook his head. "I only spoke with him on the phone. What's going on? This isn't like you to get into trouble. Since when do you gamble? I saw there's a casino in town. There's help you can get for a gambling addiction."

"I don't gamble, and I don't owe anyone money." He kept his voice low and enunciated his words. "Someone used you to get to me."

"Why?"

He held up a finger and sent a text to Frank. "It's job related."

"You into something illegal?"

"No." His voice held an edge. "Kyle, you're a good guy, but you've been duped. When you're contacted again, I need to know immediately." Frank's text gave the all clear for Kyle to stay at the house. "Come on. We need to go."

"What about our food?"

He tossed a twenty and a five on the table and stood. "That should cover it. Get the food to go, and I'll meet you outside."

Kyle rose, grumbling. "Fine."

Marc nodded and strode to his car. If Olivia was put in more danger because of him, he'd never forgive himself. But one thing really bothered him. How did they connect him with Olivia?

Carissa stood in the entryway just inside the main house with Frank, her attention divided between him and Olivia as she bounced on a pogo stick on the front porch.

"Marc has a friend who was approached and tricked into finding him." He kept his voice at a whisper.

"You think it has anything to do with Olivia?"

"It's possible. I expected trouble given the nature of

our job but not anything directed toward Marc."

"How would they know who Marc was guarding?" Carissa couldn't understand how this all fit together, but her gut told her it did.

Two cars drove onto the property. Carissa stepped outside. "Olivia, would you come inside please? I'd like to borrow that horse book you told me about."

Olivia left the toy on the porch. "It's in my room. Be right back."

"I need to go to the guesthouse," Carissa said. "Will you stay in here until I come find you?"

"Okay." Olivia charged up the stairs.

Marc opened the front door and stopped short. "I'm sorry, guys. This is my fault."

Carissa patted his shoulder. "Don't beat yourself up. There's nothing you could've done. Besides, we don't know for certain this has anything to do with our case."

"But we'll operate on that assumption," Frank said, his face grim. "Where's Kyle now?"

"I asked him to wait in his pickup."

"Good. I have plans for him. We've all stated at one time or another we need a fourth. He just dropped in our laps. Kyle may have been sent for other purposes, but if he agrees, we're going to use this situation to our advantage." Frank warned Linda to stay inside with Olivia for the time being then set the alarm for the main house and motioned for them to follow him. Once back in the guesthouse, he explained his plan.

Carissa blew air out between her lips. "That's pretty convoluted, Frank. I don't know."

"Have I ever let you down?"

"Well there was that—"

Frank cleared his throat, silencing her. "Are we all clear on how this will go down?"

Carissa nodded.

Marc frowned.

"What is it, Marc?" Carissa asked.

"I don't like using Kyle like that."

"You have a better idea?" Frank asked.

"No."

"It's your call." Frank clapped Marc on the shoulder as he strode past him. "I'm going to bed. Wake me if there's any trouble."

"What about you, Marc?" Carissa asked. "You planning on getting any sleep today?"

"I don't know, but I know one thing for sure. I don't want you alone with Kyle all day."

"Anything I should know?"

"Ladies find him irresistible."

"Funny. The same could be said about you."

The surprise on his face didn't come close to the shock reverberating through her, thanks to her flippant, but honest, comment. Ignoring her feelings got more difficult by the second.

15

Marc leaned a hip against the counter in the guesthouse while Frank explained his proposition to Kyle. Marc studied his buddy and realized the man had aged over the past year. His short hair sported a little gray in the temple area, but his brown eyes shone.

Kyle had always been cautious, never one to jump into anything without thinking it through. Maybe he wouldn't even take Frank's offer. Then again, Kyle was loyal to a fault, proven by the fact he'd come searching for him without so much as a phone call. "Frank, I'm sorry to interrupt, but there's something I need to know before you continue," Marc said.

Frank closed his mouth and nodded.

Marc turned to Kyle. "I know you said you don't trust technology, but I still don't understand why you didn't just call to check on me. It would've saved you a lot of money and time, and you wouldn't have gone through the hassle of tracking me down."

"I thought about it and figured if you were in the

kind of trouble the man suggested, then my intervention needed to be in person. Not over the phone where you could placate me with words. I wanted to see you for myself."

Frank rested his elbows on his knees. "You mean to tell me, you knew how to reach Marc, yet you drove here instead?"

"Yes, sir."

"That seals it. You're perfect for this job. What do you say? Will you join the team of Protection Inc.?"

"I need to pray and think about it first."

Frank's face split into a huge grin. "You're a believer. That's great." He stood and left the room.

Marc sat across from Kyle. "Since when are you a praying man?"

"Most of my life."

"I had no idea."

"I suppose not. I went through a rough patch this past year and decided people can think what they want. I'm not hiding my relationship with Christ."

Kyle made it sound like God was his friend. "So, what does this relationship involve?"

"You asking because you really want to know or just being polite?"

"Forget it." Marc stood. "I'm being nosey." Though he considered himself a Christian, the idea of Christ being his friend was foreign.

"Wait! I'm sorry. That was out of line." Kyle stood. "How about we go down to the beach, and I'll tell you about it?"

Marc yawned. "Maybe later. I've been up all night, and you're cutting into my sleep."

"Oh, sorry about that. Guess I'm on my own then."

"Kyle? About CJ."

"What about her?"

"She's special to me."

"Got it." Kyle gave him a look he couldn't decipher.

Marc nodded and stumbled down the hall to his bed.

The setting sun drew Carissa out to the garden. She loved how the fading light played off the Koi pond. The door to the guesthouse opened, and Marc stepped out. She waved and patted the bench.

He lumbered over and settled beside her.

His arm brushed against her shoulder sending a ripple of pleasure through her. She sat tall and tried to ignore the sensation. "How's it going with your buddy?"

"So far, fine. Did you see him today?"

"No. Frank had him in the observation room. He figured it'd be a good place for him since it was his first day."

Marc crossed his ankles and rested his arm on the seatback. His fingers grazed her shoulder. "This summer sure isn't turning out like I expected."

"How so?" Carissa couldn't tell if he was happy or

sad. His voice didn't give anything away, and the fading light made it difficult to read his face.

"For starters being a bodyguard is nothing like I expected. And this thing with Kyle. I don't even know what to think about all that. I can't imagine why anyone would involve him in this. But of all my friends, I'm glad it was him. He's someone I'd want by my side if I was in trouble." He fingered her hair.

Carissa tensed, afraid to give in to her feelings. She couldn't go there, and clearly, Marc wanted to. "Marc?"

He removed his arm and shifted to face her.

"Never mind." Why did this have to be so difficult? "How about you come to church with Frank and me on Sunday? Now that Kyle's here, you could get away."

"Doubtful. Kyle's a churchgoer, too. I imagine he'll want to attend services somewhere." He frowned.

Carissa tucked away this new information and stood. "I'm sure the two of you could work something out. Let me know if you change your mind." She took a step toward the main house.

"Carissa?" He stood and took her hand. "Is everything okay between us? I'm getting mixed signals." His voice was gentle and his eyes pleaded with her for understanding.

Carissa stood within inches of him. His warm breath tickled her cheek. She gave his hand a squeeze and released it. "I'm sorry for that. I'm your boss, Marc, and as such I need to remain professional." Her heart cracked just a bit, and she rushed to the house.

The next morning, shouts in the kitchen drew Carissa down the stairs. It sounded like Olivia was having a temper tantrum. She poked her head around the corner and spotted Linda with her hands on her hips and a scowl on her face. Olivia copied her grandmother's stance.

Linda looked toward Carissa. "Oh good, you're here." She strode toward her. "Olivia wants to go to the beach alone."

Olivia stamped her foot. "I'm not a baby, Grandma! I'm sick of hanging out with CJ. I'm old enough to be alone on the beach."

Carissa looked from grandmother to granddaughter and considered her options—side with Linda or side with Olivia. "You're right, Olivia. You aren't a baby." Carissa stepped further into the room. "But I thought you enjoyed hanging out with me. If you'd rather not, that's fine." She could guard Olivia while giving her the space she wanted.

Olivia scowled. "But I thought…"

Carissa held her breath and prayed Olivia would back down.

"I do like hanging out with you, CJ. I just like to do things by myself sometimes. I don't see why I can't go down to the beach alone."

"It's not safe." Carissa tucked a hand into her pocket.

Linda's gaze shot to Carissa.

"You know the rule to always swim with a buddy?"

Olivia nodded. "What's that have to do with me going for a walk and looking for shells?"

"The same is true for the ocean."

"I'm not going to swim."

"Will you be looking for shells in the surf?"

"Maybe…" Olivia dragged out the word. Uncertainty clouded her eyes.

"Then you need someone with you. You know we have sneaker waves in Oregon. What if one hit you, and no one was there to make sure you weren't washed out to sea? Your grandmother cares too much about you to take a risk like that."

"Oh." She looked at her grandma. "Why can't you watch for the sneaker waves while I look for shells? You never want to be with me."

Linda rushed to her granddaughter. "Oh, honey. I'm sorry you feel like I don't spend any time with you, but if you think about it, that's not true. You and I read together every day. We get our nails done and have picnics on the beach sometimes, too. But I don't have endless hours of free time." She waved toward the mess on the counter. "I have to finish baking these scones for the ladies group I'm meeting with later. But if you'll have patience and wait, I can go down to the beach with you before I leave."

Olivia's face lit into a smile. "Okay."

Carissa breathed a little easier. Another crisis

averted. One way or another, security would be close by when Olivia went down onto the beach. Looked like it was time to meet with the new guy and have him keep an eye on Olivia just this once before they introduced him to the family.

Carissa leaned against a huge driftwood log and shook her head. "Absolutely not."

"Come on." Julie propped her hands on her hips. "You know you want to."

"What I want and what I can do don't always match up. I can't surf and do my job." She motioned to Olivia. "Who's going to protect her if I'm out on the waves?" True to her promise, Linda had gone with her granddaughter to the beach but then had to leave shortly after. Kyle watched over them from a distance.

"Get one of the guys. You deserve a break."

"No. She's my responsibility."

"Fine." Julie crossed her arms. "You've changed. You used to be so much fun."

The air sparked between them. "I'm still fun, but I'm working. I don't try to get you to play hooky from work. What's gotten into you? You're being very demanding. That's not like you."

Julie's eyes widened. Then her face softened. "You're right, and I'm sorry. I've missed having my old friend to hang out with, and I know you won't be here forever. I'll try not to be so pushy. By the way, thanks for setting me up with Linda. She hired me to cater the event at the museum in October."

"You're welcome. I'm glad it worked out."

"I was hoping you might have a few other leads before then."

"Sorry, no. I don't live here anymore, remember?" Now that their business was based in Seattle, she rarely visited Lincoln City. "Don't you have some contacts? Surely, one of your former co-workers would put in a good word."

"Maybe. I could check." Julie frowned. "I was so angry when the new owner let me go, I haven't been back since or tried to keep up with anyone. Maybe my new boss will let me put out business cards for my catering business."

"That's a great idea. You could also ask Linda if she has any friends looking for a caterer."

"Good thinking." She motioned toward Olivia. "By the way, what's up with the kid? She rich or something? I realize her grandparents are, but she must be very valuable to someone for the kind of protection your company is providing."

"I can't discuss her situation."

"Why not? I won't tell anyone."

Olivia waved to them.

"It looks like I'm being summoned." She pushed off the log. "You coming?"

"Nah. Think I'll grab my board and surf."

Carissa jogged to Olivia. "What's up, kiddo?"

"I thought maybe you and Julie might want to help me build the biggest sandcastle ever." She frowned and looked to where Julie had been. "Did she leave because of me?"

"Of course not. She wanted to go surfing."

"You should've gone."

"Then who would've been with you?"

"I don't need a babysitter." Her tone sharpened. "I'm old enough to take care of myself." Her eyes pleaded with Carissa to understand. "The bad guys are in Arizona. I'm safe here."

"That may be, but I already explained, having a buddy on the beach with you is always the best. Besides, I don't feel like surfing." She held her breath.

"Well, I guess if you don't want to."

Carissa blew out her breath softly. This summer couldn't come to an end soon enough. She sure hoped the FBI would hurry up and find the people who abducted Olivia's mom. Then they could all go back to their normal lives. Unease filled her. What if the FBI never found them?

16

Carissa watched Olivia on the monitor from the observation room as she rode her bike in the driveway loop. She jiggled her leg up and down, willing Frank to wrap up the meeting. His update did little to ease the tension in her neck.

Frank continued to fill the team in on the latest intel regarding the unidentified subjects that grabbed Olivia's mother. According to Roger, she'd been blindfolded. Then they threatened to kill Olivia if his son didn't agree to give him what he was working on.

"Do we know what Olivia's dad is working on?" Kyle asked.

"Negative." Frank looked back at his notes. "Whatever it is, it's top secret, and the government is very interested in its success. I'm beginning to think we were deliberately misled as to what Olivia's parents are involved with. But that's beside the point. Our clients believe their daughter is safe in our care and want us to continue to provide protection. Meanwhile, they've been moved to a more secure location."

Carissa hadn't realized this was a government project. Not that it changed anything, but that bit of knowledge added a weight she didn't need or want. Olivia had been beyond difficult lately. She wasn't getting paid enough to protect this preteen whose moods swung like a pendulum. She glanced at her watch. "I should be getting back to Olivia. Is there anything else, Frank?" She no longer trusted the girl to stay where she was told. Olivia's independent streak almost constantly tested Carissa's limits.

"Yes. I was able to surmise that this group is highly organized and armed. I know I don't need to say it, but stay vigilant."

Marc nodded and caught Carissa's attention.

Carissa couldn't pull her gaze away from him. What was he thinking?

"Marc. CJ." Frank scowled at them. "Focus."

Carissa frowned and stood. "I'll be with Olivia." She strode from the room, trying to squash the annoyance she felt toward her partner. She did her job well and didn't need to be reprimanded.

"Carissa, wait." Marc hustled up beside her.

"What is it?" Since Frank pointed out she needed to keep her focus on the job and not allow Marc to become a distraction, she'd felt compelled to give him a wide berth, but he was making it very difficult.

"I'll come with you." He opened the door and allowed her to exit first.

She kept her focus forward and kept walking. "I know for a fact Frank is watching us, so look forward and don't react. You and I need to stay focused on the job. We have a little girl whose safety is our top priority. I can't afford any distractions. Understood?"

"I see Frank got to you. He talked to me, too, but I don't care what he thinks, and neither should you. This is between us. If we want to spend time together, let him deal with it. We can get to know one another and still do our job."

"I disagree. You may not care, but I do. Frank is my business partner, mentor, and friend."

Marc rested a hand on her arm. "Will you stop walking for a minute?"

"Marc, please. I can't do this."

"Do what?"

She looked pointedly at his hand. "I'm working. Let me do my job."

"I'm working, too. We'll watch her together. How about we all go for ice cream?"

"Weren't you listening in there? These people are determined and extremely dangerous. We should stay on the property. It's the only way to ensure Olivia's safety."

"I disagree. We can't keep her locked up here all summer. She's going to run if we don't give her a little freedom."

Carissa hesitated. He made a good point, especially in light of Olivia's rebellious attitude lately.

"Come on." He bumped her shoulder. "Live a little." Marc grinned. "Please…" He drew the word out. "I'm sure Olivia would love to get away from this place for a bit."

Maybe Marc was right. She couldn't always worry about what Frank thought. She was an adult and a professional capable of making her own choices. This was business, and they couldn't keep a ten-year-old locked up on the estate for the rest of the summer. She had to get out once in a while.

"I guess a trip to the ice cream shop would be fun."

Marc took Carissa's hand and squeezed it. "I'll let Frank know what we're doing. Will you get Olivia?"

"Sure. Are we walking or driving?"

Although he had confidence in their ability to keep Olivia safe, walking would be an added risk. "Let's drive."

Carissa nodded and strode toward the driveway where the girl still rode her bike.

Marc went to the guesthouse and found Frank in the observation room. "CJ and I are taking Olivia to Eleanor's in Siletz Bay for ice cream."

Frank shrugged. "I suppose it's okay. Just keep her close."

"Will do. We're driving. We shouldn't be gone more than an hour." He found Kyle sprawled on the couch, eyes closed. Good thing, since he was taking over the night shift. He'd offer his bed, but Kyle could sleep in the middle of a battlefield. Marc slipped out the door and found the girls in the garden. "Ready?" He pulled up short at the storm brewing in Olivia's eyes.

CJ shrugged and walked beside him to his car. Olivia dragged behind. What kid didn't love ice cream? He opened the door for Carissa and then for Olivia. "What's your favorite flavor, Olivia?"

"Chocolate mint chip."

Marc wrinkled his nose and closed Olivia's door then sat behind the wheel. He was more the rocky road type.

"I like it all." Carissa strapped on her seatbelt. "It's hard to decide which flavor to get."

"There has to be at least one flavor you don't like." Marc started the engine and pulled into the driveway. The gate opened automatically, and he pulled forward. A few empty cars were parked along the roadside— probably tourists.

Olivia leaned forward stretching the seatbelt to its max. "I don't like anything with nuts."

"I love nuts." Carissa turned toward the center of the car. "I'm racking my brain trying to think of an ice cream I don't like, and I can't come up with one. Sure, some are better than others, but they're all good."

Olivia sat back and looked out the window with a frown. Marc wished he could read her mind. One thing was clear. The kid was troubled. His stomach knotted.

Maybe a trip out had been a bad idea, and they should head back home. No. He'd promised ice cream and that's what they would get.

Marc turned right at the light and proceeded toward the parking lot. Siletz Bay was to their left and the ocean straight ahead beyond the covered picnic area. He found a spot to park and set the brake. Olivia hopped out and wandered to the backend and waited. Seagulls screeched overhead, and the air hinted at fish.

The pink building with the large mermaid off to the side beckoned them. His mouth watered. He linked his fingers with Carissa's. He was afraid she'd pull away, but when she shot him a smile, he knew they were okay—at least for now.

They all crossed the street together and walked inside. A groan escaped his lips. Where had all the people come from? Parking had been a breeze.

Carissa leaned in close. "Let's go. There's another shop a short walk from here that has ice cream."

"Too late." He pointed toward Olivia who had pushed her way to the front. He lost sight of her for a second. His gut did a somersault. He craned his neck above the crowd and stepped forward. There she was. His shoulders relaxed.

Carissa sighed. "I guess we can get our cones here, but we're not eating inside. The picnic area by the beach, or even down on the sand would be fine, but inside is definitely out. I'm going to get Olivia and bring her back here where she belongs. I'm surprised everyone let her cut like that."

Marc nodded. A commotion near the billiard table captured his attention. Apparently, some woman had just cleared the table. Pool wasn't his thing, but he respected her accomplishment.

"You'd think she won an Olympic medal or something," some guy in line beside him mumbled.

He watched the group a moment longer. At least they knew how to have fun, which was more than he could say for his group. Looking back to where Olivia had been, his heart skipped a beat. Where had she gone this time? His gaze took in the whole room. He spotted CJ, who was searching the crowd as well.

CJ squeezed through the throng of people toward him. "Do you see Olivia? When I got to the front of the line, she was gone."

"No." His gut clenched. He only wanted to make the kid happy and spend a little time with CJ. This was not supposed to happen.

"Did anyone see a girl?" CJ held her hand to Olivia's height. "About this tall with shoulder length, dark, curly hair. She's wearing a pink windbreaker."

Marc backed toward the exit. Olivia had to be in the shop. He would've seen her pass.

"Yeah. I saw her," a woman advised. "She went that way." She pointed toward the exit.

Carissa's eyes widened. "Thanks." She rushed toward Marc and the exit. "You stay here in case she comes back. I'll look outside."

Carissa's heart pounded. Why had she agreed to this? Especially since Olivia didn't want to go. She'd pulled her "I'm not a baby" shtick again and wanted to be allowed to walk up the beach alone to get ice cream by herself. What was wrong with this kid? Didn't she know girls traveled in packs?

A flash of pink caught her attention. She ran across the parking lot toward the public restrooms. "Olivia when I get my hands on you..." She slid to a stop on the sandy sidewalk and gripped the girl's shoulder. "Olivia! You know better..."

The child screamed.

Carissa snatched her hand off the girl and backed away. "I'm sorry I thought you were someone else."

"What are you doing?" A man who had at least one hundred pounds on her glowered. "Get away from her!" He looked over his shoulder and hollered. "This woman tried to grab my daughter. Someone call 9-1-1."

Carissa's eyes widened, and she raised her hands. "Whoa. That's not what's going on here."

A woman got in her face. "How dare you." She grabbed Carissa's arm and held tight.

"I didn't do anything. This is all a misunderstanding." She could easily break free from the woman's grip but escaping the mob that had formed was another matter.

A siren pealed and grew louder by the second.

Good. The sooner the authorities arrived the quicker she could be looking for Olivia and enlist their help as well. The patrol car pulled up and stopped. An officer around her own five-foot-nine frame stepped out. Although not tall, the man had shoulders like a football player. His mouth was set into a straight line, and his eyes narrowed. She didn't recognize him.

"What's the problem here?"

"This woman tried to grab that man's daughter, but don't worry. I didn't let her get away."

Carissa wanted to flick the woman off like a flea but knew any sudden movements would cause a reaction from the newbie cop. "My name is Carissa Jones, and I wasn't trying to grab his daughter. I thought she was a girl that I am taking care of. I lost her a little bit ago."

The officer squinted at her. "Let me see some I.D."

Carissa sighed. "I left my purse at the house. Look, call Sergeant Michaels. He'll vouch for me."

"You know the sarge?"

"Yes. I was on the force until I quit to open my own protection agency. I work with Frank Graham."

"I know Frank. He's a good guy." He turned to the woman who still held a death grip on Carissa's arm. "There was no harm done. Thanks for your help."

The woman's grip loosened. "Well. I guess…" She released her hold and glared at Carissa. "Fine, but you better be more careful in the future."

Carissa ground her teeth, holding back a sharp reply. Although she appreciated the woman jumping in to protect a child, she needed to learn when to back off. Instead, Carissa turned to the officer. "The girl I'm protecting disappeared. Her name is Olivia, and she's wearing a similar windbreaker." She grabbed her phone from her pocket and pulled up a photo of Olivia. "This is what she looks like. I'll send it to a few friends on the force, but since you're here, maybe you could keep watch for her."

"Sure thing." He nodded toward the dispersing crowd. "Too bad the lynch mob wasn't interested in helping."

"No kidding." Her cell went off. "Yeah."

"What's taking so long?" Anxiety laced Marc's voice. "I've been waiting here for fifteen minutes."

"Sorry. I had a minor problem. She didn't turn up inside?"

"No. You didn't find her either I gather?"

"No." She scanned the area around her. Surely, if Olivia was here, she'd have said something after what happened. Fear for the child filled her. What if someone had grabbed her? *Lord, please protect Olivia.*

17

Frank bellowed, and Carissa pulled the phone away. "Frank, listen to me! She's been missing less than twenty minutes. We'll find her. I only called to touch base in case she tries walking home. I'm heading to the beach now, and I'll look for her there." She disconnected the call before he could yell again.

She turned to Marc. "There's no sign of her, and no one I've asked has seen her. She wanted to walk to the ice cream shop from the house."

"You think she would've taken the beach instead of the road?"

"Probably. She knows that way home."

"This is my fault." Marc sighed. "If I hadn't suggested we go for ice cream…"

"We don't have time to play the blame game." She shook her head. "Sorry for snapping. Take the car and go back to the house."

"You think they took her?"

"I don't know. Keep a lookout. I sent Olivia's

picture to a couple friends of mine on the police force. Between all of us…" She took a calming breath. "I'll return to the house via the beach." Carissa didn't wait for his reply, but instead, hustled toward the sand." Pushing down rising panic she shot up another quick prayer.

Why were there so many people on the beach today? Another flash of pink caught her eye. Her pace quickened along with her heart rate until she realized it was the same girl she'd mistaken for Olivia earlier. Where is she?

"Excuse me."

Carissa turned toward a teen boy. "Yes?"

"I heard you asking about a girl with curly brown hair wearing a pink windbreaker. I saw someone matching that description a while ago running that way." He pointed toward where the bay met the ocean.

"Thanks!" Carissa angled toward the water and the solid beach surface, her feet slipping through the sand. Her arms pumped as she extended her stride, and her breath evened out as she found a rhythm.

She reached the cove at the end of the bay and followed the curve of the beach toward the crashing waves. Driftwood littered the massive area to her right and no little girls wearing pink walked the beach in front of her. She could see for quite a distance. There was no way she'd miss Olivia if she was on the beach unless she was picking her way through the tall grass. She looked to her right. Maybe just maybe Olivia was up there.

Tears pricked the back of Carissa's eyes. She headed in that direction, keeping a lookout for anyone wearing pink.

Marc drove slowly along Hwy 101. He hoped CJ would find Olivia because the child hadn't gone this way. Wouldn't they have seen someone grab her? How could Olivia disappear so fast? One minute she was there; the next she wasn't.

His cell beeped in his ear.

"You find her?" Frank asked, his voice calm.

"Not yet. I'm almost to the house. CJ's scouring the beach. When I get there, I'll start from the estate and work my way toward her."

"I haven't told her grandparents she's missing, but if we don't find her in the next thirty minutes, I'll have to. I'm praying that won't be necessary." The line went dead.

Marc's breath came out in a puff. Helplessness clung to him like barnacles on a whale. How did Carissa hold it together? Maybe this line of work wasn't for him after all. He eased up to the gate and entered the code. The gate slid open, and he pulled forward into his normal parking spot.

Double-timing it, he went to the stairwell and trotted down. About halfway from the bottom, he stopped and studied the people on the beach. "No way." A small form resembling Olivia trudged up the beach. "Olivia." He waved his arms and raced toward the girl.

She kept walking toward him, seemingly unaware of his anxiety and gave a small wave.

He jetted up to her. "Where have you been? Do you realize what a panic you caused?" He got down on his knees and gripped her arms. "Olivia, you can't wander off like that. We thought someone grabbed you."

Silent tears slid down Olivia's face, and Marc realized he'd been shouting. His stomach dropped, and he released his hold on her arms. "I'm sorry for yelling."

He calmed his shaking voice. "You need to tell us when you're leaving. Do you have any idea what could've happened to you?"

"You're scaring me. I want my mom." Her tears turned to sobs.

"Hey, buddy, leave the kid alone." A big, bald guy glowered down at him.

"Why don't you mind your own business?" Marc snapped.

"You okay?" Baldy bent over and peered at Olivia.

She flung her arms around Marc's neck and buried her face in his shoulder.

The man shrugged and walked off.

Marc patted Olivia's back until she calmed. "I need to let CJ know you're okay." He peeled off her chokehold and stood. Rather than call, he shot off a text.

Olivia hiccupped. "Is CJ mad at me?"

"Probably. You really shouldn't have done that. I thought you understood after what happened at your house."

"You mean when someone shot at us?"

He nodded.

"I thought I was safe here. I just wanted to prove to everyone that I'm not a baby. CJ wouldn't let me walk. She said it was too far, and it's not."

"You're right. It's not. But what you did was very dangerous."

"Other kids my age go out alone all the time."

"But you're not other kids."

"I am, too."

"No. You're not. Look. There's CJ."

Panting, Carissa rested her hands on her knees. "Nice to see you in one piece, Olivia. That was quite a stunt you pulled back there."

"I told you I don't need a nanny." Olivia jutted out her chin.

"For crying out loud. I'm not your nanny. I'm your bodyguard."

Olivia gasped.

"Carissa!" Marc couldn't believe she'd annihilated their cover.

"What? She's not stupid. She knew I was here to make sure she stayed safe. I'm sure she put it all together a long time ago." Carissa took Olivia's hand. "Come on. We need to have a talk."

"She had to know, Frank." Carissa crossed her arms and pleaded with her eyes for him to understand. "I realize we weren't supposed to state we were her bodyguards in so many words, but for crying out loud, the girl would have to be blind to not know what was really going on here. She was just playing along for the adults in her life."

"I disagree."

"You're wrong." She crossed her arms. "Olivia has become a danger to herself. It was time someone laid it all out for her. She needed to hear the truth in plain English. I can't keep her safe when she's always trying to slip away from me."

"Do you really think you handled that in the best way?" He scratched the back of his head. "I see a girl terrified of her own shadow. The only thing you accomplished is scaring the kid half to death."

"It's not like she didn't know someone is out to stop her dad. She's already been shot at." A small doubt festered in the back of Carissa's mind. Had she blown it? Maybe, the girl really did need the illusion of safety after what had happened. "Look, Frank. What's done is done. I know she's scared, and her grandparents are threatening to fire us, but let me talk with them."

He blew a burst of air between his lips and shook his head. "You've done enough damage. I'll deal with the family."

Carissa turned on her heel and barreled out of the observation room nearly running over Marc. "I suppose you heard?"

He nodded.

"Do you agree with him?"

"It doesn't matter what I think, but I'm concerned about you. You're taking this too personally." He reached out and touched her forearm.

She opened her mouth to protest but closed it when he pulled his hand back and tucked it into his pocket.

He kept his voice low. "I've never had the privilege of working another case with you, so I may be wrong. But I suspect you don't usually get this emotionally involved. What's different about this assignment?"

"She's a kid." Carissa's voice broke, and she blinked back tears of frustration.

Frank brushed past Carissa without so much as a nod. "Marc, I'm going to the main house. Watch the monitors while I'm gone."

"Will do, boss." Marc sent her one last look then replaced Frank.

Carissa marched to the couch and almost sat until she spotted Kyle—talk about a sound sleeper. She rerouted and parked herself on an occasional chair. Tipping her head back, she closed her eyes. Marc was right. She'd let herself get too emotionally involved. She knew better. Now Olivia was upset, and they may be fired. Then who would look out for the girl?

Carissa stood and walked back to the observation room. "You have a minute?"

Marc motioned to the chair beside him. "Have a seat."

"I need to stay focused."

He looked at her like she was speaking a foreign language.

She bit her bottom lip. "What I'm trying to say is that I really like you, Marc, but you're a distraction. I need to focus on Olivia."

"I thought we covered that already." Marc frowned. "If you're upset about what I said earlier, please don't be. I don't want my big mouth to come between us."

"It's not that. But I think you might be right. I am too emotionally involved in the case, and I need to focus on Olivia one hundred percent. I can't have any distractions and…"

"I'm a distraction."

"Exactly." She stood. "I'm sorry, Marc. I hope you understand. If Frank is able to convince them not to fire us, there will be no more trips to the ice cream store, no more private moments. We both need to stay focused." She stood and fled before he could respond.

18

Carissa sat on the window seat resting her head against the wall in her bedroom with her quilt wrapped around her shoulders. She'd found it folded and sitting outside her bedroom door. She could use a hug from her mom right now, but the quilt would suffice. She'd come upstairs after breaking up with Marc, which was crazy since they weren't even together. But here she sat with a broken heart while Frank dealt with Linda and Roger.

Maybe it was time to go back to the police force. The thing was, she felt that Olivia needed to know they were there to keep her safe and to understand that her rebellious actions could get her in trouble. Every part of her believed she'd done the right thing. Carissa set her jaw and stared out the window. Tall trees blocked the view of anything interesting. She closed her eyes.

A knock sounded on her door. She shrugged off the quilt and stood. "Come in."

Olivia poked her head inside. "It's me. Can I still

come in?"

Carissa nodded and her lips tipped up. She returned to the window seat. "Join me?"

Olivia sat and pulled her knees to her chest. "I'm sorry for leaving the ice cream store."

"I accept your apology."

Olivia's usually robust face lacked color, and her mouth drooped. "I heard Grandma and Grandpa talking. Are you going to leave? I don't want you to go."

"Why?" She needed to understand where this was coming from. "I thought you wanted your freedom."

"That was before. Now, everything's different." Olivia looked up with pleading eyes. "Don't let them send you away, CJ. I'd be so bored without you, and if my parents think I need you, then I do."

"That's very mature of you, Olivia, and I appreciate it, but it's not up to me. Your grandparents have the final say." Her heart felt a little lighter. In spite of everything, she'd been right. Olivia did need the reason Carissa was there for the summer spelled out in plain English. "Have you told your grandparents how you feel?"

"No. They were so angry. I was afraid."

"They love you very much, and they're angry with me, not you. I think you should tell them how you feel."

"I don't know."

"Trust me?"

Olivia's eyes widened, and she nodded.

"Then talk to them."

"Okay. Just don't go." She flung her arms around Carissa's neck and squeezed.

Carissa hugged her back then pried Olivia's arms free. "Whew. That was quite a hug."

"Indeed, it was." Linda walked into the room.

Olivia caught her breath. "You scared me." She sat beside Carissa. "Grandma, please don't send CJ away."

Linda shot a look of annoyance at Carissa.

"I didn't put her up to saying that."

Pursing her lips, Linda motioned to Olivia. "Come here, please."

Carissa's stomach knotted. It was clear Linda thought she'd put Olivia up to pleading her case in spite of her denial.

Olivia stood and shuffled to her grandmother.

"Good girl. Now go to your room while I talk with CJ."

Linda waited until the door to Olivia's room clicked shut then pulled the chair in the corner over to the window. "My granddaughter can be quite a handful. I appreciate all you've done this summer."

Carissa opened her mouth.

"Hear me out. Although I was angry at first, I've come to realize it was for the best. Olivia has become increasingly difficult."

Carissa's cell phone went off, and she sent it to voice mail. Julie could wait.

Linda frowned. "Frank told us about what happened at the ice cream shop, and I have to say that was shocking. But you and your team never gave up and did everything you could to find her. Thank you. Those are the kind of people we need watching out for our granddaughter. We'd like you to stay."

For the first time in hours, Carissa breathed easy. "Thank you."

Linda stood, patted Carissa's shoulder, then left the room.

Marc kept his eyes on the monitors. Everything was quiet, just the way he liked it. Tensions had cooled down substantially, including Carissa's. It seemed she meant it when she said she needed to focus on the job.

"How's it going?" Kyle eased into the chair beside him.

"Not even a blip on the screens." Marc glanced at his buddy. "What do you think of Carissa?"

"She's intense and dedicated."

"Yeah, I've noticed that myself. Before you got here, I thought we might have something going, but after the incident with Olivia, she's been...focused." He crossed his arms and frowned.

Kyle chuckled and spun toward him. "Sounds like you're jealous. You'd prefer she pay attention to you over Olivia?"

"Of course not. But we can be friendly and still do our jobs." He frowned.

"Carissa's been decent to me."

Marc's face heated. He never should've brought this up. "She's been...professional."

Kyle rested his ankle on his knee. "Sorry, buddy, but I don't see the problem." He cleared his throat. "A while back, you asked me what my relationship with Christ involved."

Marc swiveled to face him.

"You up to listening? Seems like now might be a good time."

Marc's stomach lurched. Had his skepticism shown? He was a Christian, but it seemed to him God didn't have time for everyone. If He did, wouldn't his parents still be alive? "Okay."

"I mentioned that I went through a rough patch this past year."

"Yeah. What happened?"

"My parents were killed when a drunk driver crossed the center line."

Marc blew out air between his lips. "I'm sorry. I had no idea, but you and I have that in common."

Kyle's eyes widened. "You're kidding? For real? Man, that is not something I want in common with anyone."

"I hear you. It's life altering. Why didn't you tell me?"

"I couldn't talk about it. I lost it. I didn't leave my apartment for weeks and missed so much work I got fired. I shut down—stopped living."

"Did you blame God?"

He shook his head. "You're not the first person to ask me that. I was angry, but at the person who killed them, not at God. The woman had been drinking and driving. The fault rested solely with her."

"I wish you would've called or sent me an e-mail. I'd have been there for you, and maybe you wouldn't have lost your job."

"It all worked out. It took me losing my job to get right with God."

Marc shifted uncomfortably, but he couldn't leave. He had monitor duty and was stuck. He stared quietly at the screens.

Kyle stood and clapped him on the shoulder. "Let's pick this up another time. I have a few things to do before going on duty." He left the room.

Marc sighed and stretched. He felt for his buddy—knew exactly what he was going through. Movement on camera five drew his attention. Carissa and Olivia walked away from the stairwell. They both sported swimsuits and beach towels. At least someone was having a good day.

He'd give about anything to be out there with the two of them, but Carissa had made it clear—no distractions. It irked him that she allowed Frank to control her personal life, but at the same time, he respected her work ethic.

Frank stepped into the room. "Where's Kyle? I have an idea."

19

Carissa stood at the window and watched clouds move in over the ocean. The sunny day turned dark, and a strong wind whipped through the tree limbs, bending them to the side. Good thing they'd come up from the beach when they had, or they'd have stinging sand pummeling their legs. She meandered into the library and peeked over Olivia's shoulder at the computer screen. "What are you doing?"

"I'm making a movie to show my parents what Lincoln City looks like. Check this out. I even found some photos taken from the air." Olivia clicked on several things then glanced over her shoulder with a huge smile. "You're not going to believe this!"

"Oh my goodness!" A picture of her, Marc, and Olivia on the beach lit on the screen. "Where did you find this?"

Silence.

"Olivia, please. I need to know who took this picture."

She clicked back to a web page and pointed to an unfamiliar name. "That's all I know."

Carissa typed the URL for the social media into her phone. "Thanks. I'm going to show this to the guys. Will you stay here until I come back?"

Olivia nodded. "CJ, what's wrong? You're freaking me out." A branch scraped against the side of the house, and Olivia jumped.

"Relax, sweetie. I'm sorry. I didn't mean to scare you. It's nothing you need to worry about. This picture might be a clue to something we've been trying to figure out." She turned and charged from the room.

Frank's bulky form filled the doorway to the observation room. "Have you seen Kyle?"

Marc divided his attention between his boss and the monitors. "He said something about having things to do before taking over for me."

"Is he here?"

"Must be. I haven't seen him on any monitors."

"Okay. I'll find him and be right back."

Marc spotted Carissa running across the property toward the guesthouse. "Frank. You need to see this."

Frank poked his head back into the room.

"Look." Marc pointed.

Carissa's hair whipped behind her in the growing wind.

Frank frowned and moved toward the door.

Marc followed in spite of the look Frank shot him. "What?" Marc shrugged. "I want to know what's going on, too."

The door flew open. "You guys have to see this." Carissa pushed the door closed. She held out her phone.

Marc groaned. "Technology can be a real pain in the backside."

Frank snatched the phone, looked at the screen, and shook his head. "From day one, I've struggled with Kyle's reason for coming here. What do you think the chances are Kyle was contacted because of this photo? If the wrong people saw this, they'd know Marc and Olivia were together."

"How did they identify me? It's not like my name is listed on the photo. I don't believe this picture directed anyone to me. It has to be a coincidence," Marc argued.

"Nonetheless. It could be a link in understanding why Kyle was sent to find you."

"How they connected you to that picture is irrelevant," Carissa said. "The point is, it's possible, and we need to assume they know where Olivia is. See those rocks out in the surf?"

Marc looked closer.

"Those are distinct to this section of the beach. Anyone who knows the area will be able to narrow down where this picture was taken." She took her phone from Frank and pocketed it. "Should we relocate?"

"I don't see any harm in moving her, but her grandparents will have the final say." Frank rubbed the stubble on his chin.

"You're both jumping to conclusions and possibly overreacting." Marc heard the frustration in his voice and toned it down. "I say we sit tight. Let Kyle schedule a meeting with this dude who says I owe him money. We control the situation and find out who's behind all of this."

Frank nodded. "That's what I'd been thinking until this photo, but you confirmed we need to stick with my plan." He bumped Carissa's shoulder with his arm. "See, I told you we need this guy."

Marc grinned. Frank's praise soothed like balm on sunburn.

Kyle sidled up next to him. "What's all the excitement about? I heard you from the bathroom."

Carissa pulled out her phone and went to the URL she'd saved. "Olivia found this online. We think it's possible that this is why you were asked to find Marc."

Kyle peered closely at the photo. "Hmm. Wouldn't they have to already know who Marc was to ID him?"

"Exactly." Marc crossed his arms.

"Perhaps." For the first time, since she'd barreled into the house Carissa looked doubtful. "But since the picture lists where it was taken, if the wrong people see it, they'll know what city Olivia is in."

"Let's move this meeting to the observation room." Frank strode down the hall. "I don't like not having eyes on the property." The group settled into the cramped space.

Marc wanted to disprove Carissa's theory, but she had good instincts, and he had to at least consider her opinion might be on target. It was hard to accept a stranger could figure out his identity with only a picture. Maybe they were going about this all wrong. Maybe the clue wasn't him, but rather Olivia.

What if they were surfing the web and ran across the girl's photo? They'd see her location and from there it would just be a matter of watching and doing a little recon. His stomach plunged. Had they been fooled by Kyle all along? Was he in cahoots with them? He shot a look at Frank and nodded toward the door.

Frank stood. "CJ and Kyle hang here for a bit. I need Marc for something."

Marc followed him from the room and on to the back of the house to Frank's room. "Thanks. I'm glad you caught my look."

"Couldn't miss it. What's wrong?"

"I was thinking. What if Kyle is the inside man? Let's say they found Olivia's picture online then came to town and did some recon. They discovered who I am and dug a little deeper. Kyle came up as a friend and a mole is born."

Frank paced to the window and back. "You're killing me, Marc. You vouched for him. He checked out. What you're suggesting is…"

"Possible." Marc finished for him. "And if he is

working for the other side we can use him to our advantage."

Frank shook his head. "He checked out. My sources are impeccable."

"But not infallible. What if they missed something?"

Frank lowered his voice. "Do you really think Kyle is a plant?"

Marc rubbed the back of his neck and squinted. "I can't say for sure. Until that picture, I would've said no, but somehow a person who doesn't know me connected Olivia to me. I'm the weakest link. It makes sense I'd be targeted instead of you or Carissa."

Frank frowned. "Okay. Let's keep this on the down-low. I don't want to spook him if you're right. For the record, I think you're wrong, but we can't afford to make a mistake."

Marc hoped he was wrong, too. A deep-seated need to trust his friend took root in him, but he'd already cast suspicion on Kyle. They had to follow up. He settled back on his heels and listened to Frank's plan.

"Let's test Kyle and see what happens. If he's a mole, we'll use him to our advantage. If not then he'll be none the wiser."

Marc couldn't argue with Frank's reasoning. Time to institute Operation Oust. They returned to the observation room. Kyle and Carissa were both watching the monitors.

"That's quite a summer storm brewing outside."

Kyle swiveled when they stepped into the room. "You guys missed it. A tree split in two over on the north end of the property."

"Did it clear the house?"

"Thankfully." Carissa shivered.

"You cold?" Marc shrugged off his canvas jacket and laid it over her shoulders.

"Thanks."

Frank cleared his throat. "Kyle, call back the man who contacted you. Set up a face-to-face at the aquarium in Newport."

Kyle pulled out his cell and punched in the number. "It's Kyle. Do you still want to meet?"

Marc watched his friend for any sign of deception.

Kyle caught his eye and raised a brow.

His buddy knew him too well. He averted his eyes.

Kyle pocketed his phone. "Done. We'll meet at noon tomorrow."

Unease settled over Marc. The trap was laid, but who would step into it remained to be seen. He hoped it wouldn't be his friend.

Carissa stood and brushed past him. "You have a minute?" She grasped his arm and gently pulled him from the room. "Walk me back to the main house?"

"Sure." This was odd, especially after the way she'd been acting toward him. He pulled open the door. The wind almost ripped it from his grasp.

Carissa looped her arm through his and hunkered down. They ran to the front porch of the main house.

The wind was less intense there since the walls blocked its force. "What's going on? You and Frank are up to something."

"How'd you know?" He stuffed a hand in his jeans pocket.

"I'm not sure, but I picked up on it when Kyle was on the phone."

"Talk to Frank."

She crossed her arms. "I want to hear it from you."

Several locks of hair had escaped her ponytail and blew across her face. He fingered the damp hair and pushed it behind her ears. "Relax. You know they're watching, and if you look angry with me, there will be questions."

She dropped her arms to her side. "Sorry. I forget about the cameras once in a while."

Marc's jacket about swallowed up her thin frame. He took a step closer and pulled up the zipper. He wanted to draw her close and kiss her but suspected she'd lay him flat in spite of the tender look in her eyes. Instead, he led her to the stone bench. "Sit with me, and I'll explain." He drew her into an embrace making sure to turn his face away from the camera. She stiffened and he sighed. "Relax, Carissa. Kyle reads lips. I don't want him to see what I'm about to say."

Common sense told Carissa to push Marc away, but if

what he suggested was true, then it was best she allow him to hold her. Truth be known, with each passing second, she melted just a little bit more. At this rate, she wouldn't be able to resist her attraction to him. Then again, maybe she didn't want to. She closed her eyes nuzzling his cheek and breathed in deeply a hint of spice as he whispered their plan.

He leaned back.

Her eyes popped open.

"You okay?"

"Yes." She unzipped his jacket and handed it back. "Thanks. See you tomorrow." Heat burned her cheeks, and she fled to her bedroom.

Marc shrugged on his jacket and sniffed. He'd never noticed her vanilla perfume, but the collar now held the faint scent, and it warmed him to his toes. He did a scan of the property before jetting back to the guesthouse.

The wind about ripped the door from his hand.

Frank's sour face greeted him. "What was that all about?"

Marc ignored the question and closed the door. "Is Kyle on the monitors?"

"Yes, and I'm heading to the main house for the night." Frank spoke into Marc's ear as he passed. "Kyle's been dependable on the monitors so far. For now, I still trust him."

Marc nodded. Even if Kyle were a mole, he'd do his job to maintain his cover. As long as he thought he was undetected, they could depend on him to keep watch. Of course, things might be very different by this time tomorrow.

20

Marc slipped on sunglasses and walked Kyle to his car. The peaceful morning shone bright after last night's storm. "You know the plan, right?"

"We've been over it enough, yes." Kyle squinted at him. "What's going on? You seem...off."

"Just want this to go down without any problems."

Kyle grinned. "You and me both." He ducked his head and settled into his pickup. "Stop worrying." He started the engine and saluted before driving away.

Five minutes later, Marc slid into Frank's car. They left the property and followed the same route Kyle had taken. In less than an hour, they'd know if Kyle was a mole.

"Yeow!" Carissa dropped the pan onto the counter. "Oh, that hurts." She flipped on the faucet and placed her arm under the cold water.

"What happened?" Olivia studied Carissa's hand.

"I bumped the cookie sheet with my wrist."

"Ouch."

"Exactly."

Julie squeezed between them. "Let me see." She gently inspected the burn. "You'll live. It'll probably only leave a small red mark."

"These cookies better be worth it."

"They are." Julie moved the treats onto a cooling rack. "Where are the men? One of them is always hovering nearby."

Carissa shut off the water. "They're running an errand."

"Sounds ominous. I can't imagine what kind of errand would require hulking men."

"Maybe they're getting furniture." Olivia snatched a cookie and blew on it. "When we moved, lots of men came to put our furniture into the truck."

"I could probably fit everything I own into the bed of a pickup."

"Really, Julie? The last time I was at your place it was completely furnished."

"I had to sell a few pieces when I was between jobs."

"Oh." What did a person say to news like that? Everything that came to mind sounded trite. "Well, if you need anything, let me know. I may be able to help."

"You've already been a huge help. I talked to Linda like you suggested, and I've had a couple requests from

186

her friends. They're small jobs, but I'm really looking forward to them."

"That's wonderful." Carissa snagged a cookie for herself and poured a glass of milk. "Would either of you like any?"

"Sure," they said at the same time.

She poured two more glasses and placed them on the table. "Break time, girls."

"So really, where are the guys?" Julie bit into a peanut butter cookie and sat beside Olivia.

Carissa sighed. "What's the big deal?"

"You're just being so mysterious about it. I'm curious."

"Well, there are some things I can't talk about." Nor would she mention Frank's buddy he'd called in who sat out in the guesthouse filling in on the monitors.

"Fine." Julie pushed back from the table and stood. "I'll get the final batch out and be on my way."

"You don't need to leave." Carissa swallowed the last of her milk and carried the glasses to the sink.

"I have to work."

"Oh." She glanced at Olivia, who rolled her eyes. Carissa stifled a giggle.

"Would the two of you mind cleaning up this mess?" Julie swept her arm in front of her. "I really need to get going."

"Sure, no problem." Carissa walked her to the door. "What's going on? You didn't mention work earlier. I thought you planned to spend the day with us."

"I got a text that the cook working today needs to

go home sick." Julie reached for the door and pulled it toward her. "We'll have to do this again sometime soon. Olivia is a doll."

"Okay. I'll see you." Carissa waited at the door until the gate closed then returned to the kitchen unable to shake that something was up with Julie.

Marc sat in the car watching the line dwindle as hyper kids and their parents filtered into the aquarium. A lone man, wearing jeans and a hoodie walked to the entrance and disappeared inside. Marc sent a text to Frank to be on the lookout. That had to be the guy meeting Kyle.

He counted to twenty, made sure the stuffed belly he wore was situated right, and pulled his baseball cap low, then followed. Hopefully, the disguise would work. The man stood about five people ahead of him in line. All he had to do was avoid detection while taking pictures and observing the meet. If Kyle was up to no good, it'd be clear soon.

The man walked to the estuary trail where Kyle waited. Frank hid in the foliage nearby where he'd hear everything the two said. Marc pulled out his smartphone and clicked away. Kyle and the man ignored him as he passed and didn't seem to notice he'd snapped their picture at least a half-dozen times. He continued to the end of the trail before turning back. Hopefully, Frank had heard an earful.

A family meandered along the trail, but Kyle was gone. Time to hustle. He skipped having his hand stamped for readmission and booked it to Frank's car. "How'd it go?"

"Looks like your buddy is on the up and up. The conversation was brief, but from what I gathered, Kyle's been telling us the truth."

Marc leaned his head back, and a smile curved his lips. He pulled the padding from under his shirt and tossed it onto the backseat. "I'm glad to be rid of that thing." But more importantly, he was happy his buddy wasn't a traitor.

Frank started the engine and pulled forward. "Kyle is only a few minutes ahead of us, but he may be in danger. I think someone's following him."

Marc sat taller. "Who?"

"The guy he met inside the aquarium. He never revealed his name, but I suspect once we run those photos through face recognition, we'll come up with something. The man oozed trouble."

Marc scoffed. "So do you, but I don't hold that against you." He grinned. "Why do you suppose he's being followed? It doesn't make sense."

"I agree. He could try to figure out where you are. Maybe he's tailing Kyle hoping he'll lead him to you."

"Considering I was supposed to be with him, that makes sense." They crossed over the Yaquina Bay and drove through downtown Newport.

Marc pointed. "Look. There's Kyle's pickup, and he's not inside."

Frank passed by the parked vehicle and pulled into the next available spot about a half block away. "You see him?"

"No." He checked the side mirror and looked all around. "You think he's in jeopardy?"

"Maybe. Or he could've spotted one of us at the aquarium and is having a second meeting now. Your disguise was good, but not perfect."

Marc's stomach dropped. "Want me to look for him?"

"Too risky. We'll stay put and wait for him to return. I don't see his tail."

"Me, either, but he could've parked on a side street."

Frank's mouth stretched into a straight line. "I hadn't anticipated this. Send the pictures to CJ. She can at least get started on identifying the man."

Marc sent the best photos. "You must have some serious connections."

Frank slid low into his seat. "There he is."

Marc glanced in the mirror and spotted Kyle with a takeout bag in his hand. "Maybe he only stopped to get a bite. It's not like he knew we were following him."

"Could be." Frank started the engine and waited for Kyle.

"Why aren't you going?"

"Just wait."

A black SUV pulled out of a side street. "That's the man he met with." Marc punched the license number into his phone and sent it to Carissa.

190

"Time to roll." Frank pulled out.

Marc's phone rang. "Carissa. Talk to me."

"I ran the plate you sent. It's a rental."

"Do we have a name?"

"I called, but they wouldn't give it to me."

"Okay. Any hits in the facial recognition software?"

"Not yet."

Marc stifled a groan. "Okay. We'll be back in about thirty minutes, barring no more surprises." He disconnected the line and turned to Frank. "She's got nothing."

"I gathered. Some things take more time than we'd like, but one way or another, we'll figure this out. My immediate concern is that Kyle will lead his tail back to the house. Hang on." He floored the accelerator and weaved around the car in front of him.

Marc's heart pounded. "It's not legal to pass here."

"Trust me. I know what I'm doing." Another break in oncoming traffic prompted Frank to downshift.

White knuckled, Marc gripped the seat.

Frank passed two vehicles, including the mystery man, then slowed.

Kyle's car pulled further away, and they lost sight of him.

"Mission accomplished. His tail won't be following either of us back to the estate." Frank increased his speed to the limit.

Marc took a full breath for the first time since Frank started his crazy driving. "I don't think I'm cut out for this."

"Hang with me long enough, and you'll get used to it."

"Never." A lot of good any of this did. They were no closer to knowing the truth about Kyle than they were before this day began.

Frank drove past the gate and parked on the far side of the property. "Let's make a run for the back door. Maybe Kyle won't notice."

"He will if he's on the monitors."

Frank slid open the back door and held a finger to his lips. They slunk to the observation room and stalled in the doorway. "Thanks, John. We got it from here."

"Great. Everything was quiet." John waved and sauntered out the door.

"Kyle's car is in the driveway." Marc pointed. "He's coming out of the main house."

"Looks like CJ bought us some time." Frank pushed him down into the seat and left the room.

A few minutes later, Kyle leaned against the doorframe. Marc swiveled to face him. "How'd it go? What'd you find out?"

"Let's wait for Frank, and I'll fill you both in together." He handed over a baggie holding four cookies. "The girls baked."

21

Carissa sent Olivia to her room then two-timed it to the guesthouse. She flung the door open and smacked Frank in the shoulder. "Sorry."

"No harm done." Frank lowered his voice. "Any hits on the photo?"

"Negative. I wouldn't count on anything coming of the pics. The guy probably used prosthetics to hide his true identity from Kyle."

"Yeah." He nodded toward the observation room. "Join us?"

"I wouldn't miss this for anything." Carissa followed him to the room.

"Thought I heard voices," Kyle said.

Frank plopped into an empty chair. "What did you find out?"

"Not much. I told the guy that Marc denied owing him money and suggested he had the wrong man. He took a call and then said I was right and bolted out of there."

"That's it?" Marc crossed his arms. "He let it go?"

"Yep. I don't know who was on the other end of the call, but apparently, it was a game changer."

Frank rubbed his chin. "Interesting. What'd you do after that?"

"I stopped for lunch then came straight back."

Silence.

Carissa fought the battle raging in her head. If Kyle was telling the truth, then they were no closer to understanding why he'd been sent to them. Now she had even more questions. Time to get some answers. A glance in Frank's direction suggested he was as determined as she to get to the bottom of this.

Frank caught her attention and nodded. She pointed to herself and narrowed her eyes. They'd done good cop bad cop more times than she could remember. She excelled at bad cop.

"Kyle, join Frank and me at the kitchen table." She waited for Kyle to stand then led the way and pointed to a chair. She settled onto the seat across from him and folded her hands on the glass tabletop. "I'm going to be straight with you. Some things don't add up."

Kyle shot a glance toward Frank, who didn't offer any encouragement.

"I believe you're consorting with the guys who're after Olivia." Carissa watched Kyle's reaction closely.

His eyes widened, and his lips turned down. "You're wrong." He pushed back from the table and rose.

194

"Sit!" Carissa stood, braced her arms on the table, and leaned toward him. "Why were you followed from the aquarium, and why did you stop in Newport?" She fired the words in rapid succession. "I think you spotted Marc or Frank at the aquarium, and you needed a safer place to talk."

"No." He looked at Frank. "You can't believe this nonsense?"

"Of course not, but I've learned to let CJ voice her opinion." He winked. "Life flows better that way."

Kyle crossed his arms. "For whom?" He took a deep breath and let it out in a puff. "What can I do to convince you I'm on your side?"

Marc tried to focus on the monitors, but his attention was drawn to Carissa's voice. He'd never heard her use that tone. The woman must've been deadly in an interrogation. A visitor came to the gate. He pressed the intercom. "Julie, you're back. Carissa isn't available right now."

"I can wait. I was rude to her earlier, and I'd like to make nice."

He pushed a button and the gates opened. "Wait in the garden."

"Thanks. Hey, you want to keep me company?"

"Sorry. Can't." Something about her tone sent a chill up his spine, but he ignored it and focused instead on the conversation in the other room. It didn't sound good for his buddy. But he trusted Carissa and Frank to do the right thing. They had proven over and over to be competent and honest. Kyle was in good hands regardless of his innocence or guilt.

Julie walked from her car to the garden and sat on the bench. She jiggled her knee up and down and kept looking around. She must be really nervous about facing Carissa and based on what he was hearing from the other room, she had good reason.

Silence in the house drew him from his thoughts. What had happened? A knock sounded on the doorframe. He swiveled and faced Frank. "Well?"

"I can't be certain, but I think he's on the up and up."

"What makes you think so?"

"CJ couldn't break him. She did a good job, too. From what I was able to piece together, I'd say he's the victim of circumstances. He's not a mole."

Frank had a point. The old adage "trust no one" trotted through his mind, but he knew in his gut Kyle was one of the good guys. Marc breathed a sigh and sank deeper into the seat. "That's a relief. But you said you weren't certain."

"It's impossible to be one hundred percent positive about anyone. Don't you think?"

"Maybe." Marc turned back to the monitor and spotted Julie again. "Julie's here. Mind if I let Carissa know?"

Frank sat in the other chair. "Fine. I'll take over for a while."

Marc found Carissa in the kitchen with a cup of coffee. "How can you drink that so late in the day?"

She'd religiously visited her beloved espresso machine and made a cup every morning. "I'll probably regret it later. But after the day I've had, it was necessary."

He scooted past her and opened the fridge. A lone can of soda sat on the top shelf. He grabbed it and popped it open. "Must've been pretty bad. Julie's in the garden."

Carissa looked at him over the rim of the cup. "Really? How long has she been waiting?"

"Five or ten minutes."

She dumped the coffee into the sink.

He raised his brows.

She shrugged. "It probably would've kept me up all night anyway." After rinsing the cup, she placed it in the dishwasher and breezed outside.

The energy in the room zapped away with her departure and left him feeling empty and alone. Why? He'd had a life before CJ. But something had changed for him since they'd met and now when she wasn't around, something was missing.

Kyle strode into the room and stopped when he spotted him in the kitchen. "Oh, I didn't know you were in here."

"No worries. The space is big enough for two."

Kyle grunted and moved past him to the fridge. "You took the last soda."

"Sorry."

Kyle slammed the fridge and rounded on him. "If you had doubts about my loyalty, why didn't you just ask?"

Marc shook off the regret that swept through him. "I couldn't. Olivia's life rested in finding out the truth. What if you had been working for the people who're after Olivia, and I let you know we doubted you? What then?" He wanted—no needed—Kyle to understand that he didn't take any of this lightly.

Kyle's shoulders slumped a little, and he nodded. "I get it, but I don't like it."

"For what it's worth, I wanted to believe you were the real deal."

A slow grin spread across Kyle's face. "Whew, I'm glad we got that out of the way." He slapped Marc on the shoulder. "I'm starved. Being interrogated made me hungry. How about pizza?"

Marc chuckled. "Sure. My treat." At least Kyle didn't hold a grudge. Things could've been bad between them. "Question."

"Hmm."

"If I were in your place I probably would've decked me. What gives?"

"I was angry at first. But I let it go."

"Just like that?"

"No, but almost. God reminded me that I need to see things from your perspective."

Marc blinked. "Seriously?" God really did care about the little things.

Carissa spotted Julie on the bench and slowed her pace. She didn't feel much like talking, but short of being rude, she didn't have a choice. She squared her shoulders and marched over to her friend. "Hey. I thought you had to work."

She shrugged and patted the space beside her. "I was hoping we could talk."

Carissa sat and crossed her legs. "What's up?"

"I wanted to apologize for earlier. After I left, I realized how inconsiderate it was to take off so abruptly and leave you to clean up everything."

"Don't worry about it. How was work?"

"Fine. Where's Olivia? I thought the two of you were attached at the hip."

"Inside with her grandmother." She glanced at her watch. "They're probably reading." Carissa eyed Julie's hands, which she fiddled in her lap. Julie had always been a little high-strung, but lately, she seemed more so. Better get to the bottom of it.

"What's going on? You haven't been yourself this summer."

"Really?" Julie's voice rose in pitch. "I hadn't noticed. The same could be said of you."

Carissa crossed her arms. She wasn't going to talk

about herself. Julie would not distract her. Something about her friend's response made her uneasy. Almost anyone would be uptight given the same circumstances. If Carissa had to sell off stuff simply to survive, she'd definitely not be herself. But Julie usually flowed with life like a fishing boat on calm water. Something was going on besides her employment situation, and the sooner Carissa figured out the problem the better.

22

Carissa spotted Marc at the cliffside. It had been two days since everything went down with Kyle, and she hadn't spoken much with either man since. Time to remedy that, at least somewhat. She strode to Marc and tucked her hands into her windbreaker pockets. "How's it going?"

"Great! Better than ever actually."

That was a first. Usually, he was moderate in his replies, especially of late. "Why's that?"

He chuckled. "Am I such a sourpuss that you have to ask?"

She grinned. "I plead the fifth. But what gives? You're in a good mood."

"I suppose you're right. Kyle helped me understand a few things, and I guess it put me in a good mood."

Carissa grinned. "Do tell."

Marc explained how Kyle had told him about a bunch of stuff he'd gone through and talked to him about God. "I've been a Christian most of my life, but I was lacking the relationship that Kyle kept talking about. After my parents died and life got tough, I convinced myself that God didn't love us enough to care about small things."

She nodded. He'd stated something similar to her. "And now?"

"Now I realize that I was being blind. He's been there all along, but I wasn't paying attention. I'm paying attention now."

"Good." Carissa couldn't fathom God not caring about His creation. "I have my issues. Anyone who knows me will tell you that, but for whatever reason, since I became a Christian trusting that God was looking out for me and that He cared about all things related to us never came into question."

"Why do you think that is?"

"One of the first things I remember learning in church was that He's all-powerful, all-knowing, and everywhere. A God who knows everything and can be in multiple places at once must have the ability and desire to care about the little things."

"Kyle said something similar then pointed out some places in the Bible for me to see what he was talking about. Anyway, for the past two days I've been reading Kyle's Bible and realized I needed the kind of peace in my life that I see in the three of you. So I rededicated my life to Christ. Kyle's been a big help."

"Double wow. That's awesome. I'd like to run an

idea by you. Frank and I have our hands full with Protection Inc., and we've talked about bringing in another partner. I realize you're new at this, but you've learned a lot in a short time, and you've proven to be dependable and capable of making split-second decisions. Those are qualities we need in a partner. If you're interested, I'd like to talk to Frank."

"Wow. Talk about unexpected. Ever since I left the military, I've felt a disconnect. I didn't know where I belonged or what I was supposed to be doing with my life. I guess you could say I was searching for something, but I didn't know what." He stuffed a hand into his pocket. "I think I might now. I'm definitely interested."

"Excellent." Carissa sensed there was more to the story than he was sharing but didn't want to push him for details beyond what he was comfortable with. She desperately wanted to hug him but held back. "Where's Frank?"

"Guesthouse."

"I'll catch up with you later." She strode across the driveway, through the garden, and into the guesthouse. "Frank."

He came into the hall from the bedroom. Dark circles rimmed his eyes. "What's wrong?"

"Nothing. Did I wake you?"

"No just going over some papers." He held up a file. "I'm glad you're here. I need to talk with you about something." He slid past her and walked into the family room.

"What's going on?"

He sat on the sofa. "I want to talk with you about Marc. I've been very impressed with him. As you know, this company is growing fast, and if we're going to continue to cover so much territory, we need another partner. What do you think about asking him?"

Carissa's jaw dropped. "Did you overhear the conversation I just had with Marc?"

"No. Why?"

"I literally asked him if he was interested in joining us as a business partner."

"Without talking to me first?" Confusion laced his voice.

"I guess so. I'm sorry. We'd already talked about the need before we started this job. But you can't get mad considering you hired him without even consulting me first. I only asked him what he thought."

Frank chuckled. "Relax. We're good, CJ. As it turns out, we're both on the same train of thought. I took the liberty of having Roger draw up a contract.

Carissa gasped. "You're kidding? Without even talking to me first."

He raised a brow. "Excuse me, but aren't you the one who spoke with him before consulting me? All I did was have a contract written up. Roger did it for free." He held out a file. "Check this out. Tell me what you think."

Carissa took the papers and studied them for a few minutes. They'd divide the business into thirds. "Equal partners?" She set the contract aside since the rest of the words were a bunch of legal mumbo-jumbo.

Frank's eyes gleamed, and with sudden clarity, Carissa knew exactly what he was up to.

"What do you think?"

"I think you're a hopeless romantic and a good business man. Shall we present this to Marc and see what he says?"

Frank's face turned red. "I'll let you."

"Nope. We do this together. We're a team." She never imagined things would work out like this when Frank had first brought on Marc.

Marc heard footsteps behind him and turned. Frank and Carissa walked side by side, and they looked nervous. His gut tightened. What happened now? "Please don't tell me you have bad news."

Carissa held something in her hand and her face shone. "I hope you don't think it's bad." She held out a file.

He looked at the folder and opened it up. A contract to join Protection Inc. as a partner sat inside. His pulse leapt. "That was fast."

Frank cleared his throat. "We at Protection Inc. don't believe in wasting time."

"My kind of people. I'm humbled and honored to accept your offer." A slow grin spread across his face.

Frank motioned for the contract in his hand. "Once you've looked it over and signed it, be sure to get it back to me. After we finish this job and get back to Seattle, we'll talk details. We have some big ideas for this company. I better relieve Kyle." He turned and headed back to the guesthouse.

Carissa's eyes sparkled with excitement and dare he hope also with desire. She took a step closer to him.

"CJ. Grandma wants you." Olivia called from the front porch.

She sighed. "That girl has rotten timing."

Marc pushed down his own frustration at the interruption. "Maybe you should see what she wants."

Carissa stepped close to him and planted a kiss on his cheek. "I'm really glad you're joining us."

"Me, too." He placed his hand behind her back and drew her close. He slowly lowered his mouth to hers. Her soft lips tasted of chocolate. Her arms circled his neck, and he deepened the kiss.

"CJ!"

He groaned and released her. "You better go see what they want."

"Right." She turned and jogged toward the house, but not before he noticed her flushed cheeks.

A minute later his cell buzzed in his pocket. He pulled it out and read the text from Carissa. *Meet me at the cliff stairwell tonight at nine.*

Carissa, Olivia, and Julie sat around the dining room table playing Payday, Olivia's new favorite board game. Linda and Roger had an event this evening and would be home late. Julie finished her turn and stood. "I'm starving. How about I make a bowl of popcorn and get some soda?"

"Yes!" Olivia bounced in her seat. "I love that you guys are playing with me. This is so much fun. Grandma and Grandpa never let me stay up this late."

"Make sure it's caffeine free." Carissa tossed the die onto the board.

"Got it." Julie left the room, and a few minutes later, the whir of the air popper filled the kitchen.

Carissa looked at her watch and stifled a sigh. She'd allowed Olivia to stay up late since Julie had stopped in. Julie wanted to have a game night like they'd had as teens, and there was no getting Olivia to sleep after they started playing. "Once this round is over, you need to head to bed."

"I want to stay up with you and Julie."

"Sorry, but you need to sleep, and Julie will be leaving soon." She refused to miss her rendezvous with Marc. She touched the tip of her finger to her lips. No man had kissed her like that—ever.

"Here we go." Julie placed a tray on the table and passed out the bowls and cups.

"I love root beer." Olivia took a long gulp.

Carissa chuckled and held the cup to her mouth. She'd always had an affinity for this beverage. Her eyes widened. She coughed.

Julie leaned toward her. "You okay?"

"Fine, just the bubbles tickling my throat." Carissa took her turn and slid the die toward Olivia. The child's eyes drooped, and she looked sleepy. "Oh my goodness. It looks like I shouldn't have allowed her stay up so late." She stood. "Come on, Olivia. Time for bed."

Julie pushed back from the table. "How about you get her bed ready, and I'll carry her up."

"You sure?"

"Of course. We'll be right behind you."

Carissa took the stairs two at a time and swung open Olivia's bedroom. Stuffy air smacked her in the face. She went to the window and slid it open a few inches. A little fresh air would do this room wonders. Next, she tackled the bed and piled all the extra pillows onto the window seat. Tonight had been fun, but she was eager to meet Marc. Where was Julie? They should've been up here by now.

"Julie?" She called in a stage whisper. A niggling sense of foreboding urged her back downstairs. The front door was open, and Julie stood at the back of the van with a catering cart. "What are you doing? Where's Olivia?"

The floorboard behind Carissa creaked. Prickles ran up her spine, and she tensed. She whirled around. Everything went black.

23

Marc sat in the observation room visiting with Kyle. Everything had been quiet after Julie's arrival, although she'd left her minivan parked directly in front of the porch. Kind of annoying but not a big deal. Hopefully, she'd be leaving soon. He didn't want to wait any longer to see Carissa.

The front door opened and Julie stepped out. "Looks like Julie's leaving." Kyle pointed to the monitor.

"About time. She's been over there for hours."

Anxiety coursed through Marc. "Yeah. I know. Speaking of hours, you mind taking over now? I'd like to shower before meeting Carissa."

Kyle stuck his nose in the air and sniffed. "Romance is in the air." He waggled his brows. "Or is that sweat?"

"Very funny." Marc pushed up. "I owe you." He hustled to the bedroom, grabbed a fresh T-shirt and jeans, and then made quick time in the bathroom. Ten minutes later, he popped into the observation room. "I'm heading out. Everything look good?"

"Yep. Julie just left." Kyle swiveled to face him. "It was kind of weird though. After you left, she brought out a large rolling cart, the kind used in food service, with a long tablecloth over it and took it into the house. Then a minute later she pushed it back outside. The tablecloth must have blown off and onto the camera because I lost visual until she removed it."

"Odd." Marc didn't want to think about Julie though. In a few minutes, they'd have a shift change, and Carissa would be free.

Frank strolled past. "Hey guys. Everything quiet?"

"Yes."

"Good. I'm relieving CJ. See you in the morning."

Marc walked out with Frank. "Tell her I'll be waiting in the garden instead. It's more protected from the wind than the cliffside where she wanted to meet."

"Sure thing." Frank stopped. "You two worked things out?"

"What do you mean?"

"On a personal level."

He nodded, happy Frank had missed their private moment earlier. With all the cameras, this property left little space for a secret rendezvous.

"Good." He strode toward the main house.

Marc sat on the bench and stretched his legs crossing them at the ankles. Things had sure turned around for him over the past few days. His cell buzzed in his pocket.

"They're gone!" Frank's voice held uncharacteristic panic.

Marc's heart tripped. He bolted up, ran to the house, and burst through the front door. "What do you mean they're gone?"

"When I didn't see CJ, I went up to her room and knocked on the door. She didn't answer so I peeked inside. Her bed is made, and there's no sign of either of them."

"That doesn't make sense. What about Olivia's room?"

"Negative. But the window was open, and the bedcovers were turned back."

Marc brushed his hand across the back of his neck. "Kyle said Julie left just before I got out of the shower. She had a catering cart, but he lost visual because a cloth flew up and covered the camera."

"I want to see that footage."

"Maybe they all went out together." That had to be it. The alternative was more than Marc could accept.

"No. Carissa wouldn't take Olivia out this late. And she wouldn't leave a window open. Second level or not." Frank strode to the door with Marc on his heels.

Carissa's head hurt and so did just about every other part of her body. She groaned and opened her eyes. Her arms stretched behind her and her wrists were tethered together with a tightly bound rope. The last she remembered was seeing Julie outside the house and then…someone had knocked her out.

She looked around the space. A bed was centered on hardwood flooring up against a yellow wall. But other than that, the room was bare. There had to be a window somewhere. She craned her neck to see behind her and observed curtains. Wherever she was, it wasn't Linda's house. Voices coming from the other side of the door rose to a shout.

"I told you Carissa saw me." Julie's voice shook. "If Joe hadn't knocked her out, we would've never gotten the kid."

"You shouldn't have brought her here!" a male with a gruff voice shouted. "What are we going to do with that woman?"

"If I'd left her behind, she would've tracked us down. I had no choice."

"What have you done, Julie?" Carissa whispered.

"The important thing to remember is we have the girl. Now we get our money and leave the country like we've planned all along."

"No. You're done calling the shots," the man growled.

Silence stretched and then a scream. Something or someone was being dragged across the floor, and it sounded big. The door to the bedroom opened, and Julie stumbled in, stopping at the foot of the bed. Blood trickled from her nose. The door clicked shut and a lock slid into place.

"You can't do this to me!" Julie screamed. "This was my plan. You need me." She sat on the floor, pulled her knees to her chest, and buried her head in her arms. Her shoulders shook.

"Julie, where's Olivia?"

Julie ignored her.

"Hey!"

She looked up with bloodshot eyes. "What difference does it make?"

Carissa's heart pounded. She'd failed. Olivia was in trouble, and she couldn't help her. She'd promised herself the day her mom was mugged that no one would ever get the drop on her again. She took self-defense courses and had excellent training to back up that commitment. Protecting others was not only her job. It was her identity.

The restraints on Carissa's wrists dug into her skin. Traitor or not, she needed Julie's help. "Julie, listen to me. I'll get us out of here, but first, I need to get my hands free."

"Not a chance. You'll kill me. I'll take my chances with my team."

"You're wrong. I won't kill you. I want justice."

"Whatever. No thanks. Give up, Carissa. You can't save Olivia."

"But I have to." Failure was not an option.

Julie shook her head and pursed her lips. "You're too late."

"I thought we were friends. Friends don't do this to each other." Maybe it was the bump on the back of her head or she was dense, but none of this made sense. How had she been so wrong about Julie?

Julie sneered. "This isn't about you. It's about money—lots." She flicked a quick glance at the door. "Why'd you have to come downstairs? Another minute, and I'd have been gone. I wouldn't be in this mess if you'd only—"

Carissa tuned out Julie's words and focused on getting free. Clearly, Julie would be no help. The door opened and closed again. "Olivia!"

The frightened girl ran to her and flung her arms around Carissa's shoulders. "CJ."

Carissa leaned away from the child whose breath smelled of vomit. "Are you sick?"

"I was. But I'm better now." Olivia glared at Julie and pointed. "The man said she gave me something that made me sleep. When I woke up, I was super sick."

Julie stood, turned her back on them, and plopped down on the side of the bed out of view.

Olivia walked behind Carissa and started tugging on the ropes holding her in place.

Hope surged in Carissa's heart. "Can you loosen the knot?"

"I'm trying, but it's tight."

"Just keep working on it."

Julie peeked over the bed with dispassionate interest. "You're wasting your time, Olivia. That knot could secure Houdini."

Olivia kept at it. "I hate you, Julie! You're nothing but a liar."

Carissa winced as the rope rubbed the flesh on her wrist raw. "Take a break, Olivia." At this rate, she'd have no skin left. She had a small knife stuffed in the sole of her shoe. As a precaution, she'd cut a hole into the thickness of the side of the heel and stuffed it there for emergencies. This qualified, but if Julie was determined to see her fail, she'd probably rat her out.

Julie continued to peek her head over the top of the bed and sneered at them from across the room. "Like I said, a waste of time."

She thought she knew Julie, but this was not the woman she'd been friends with for years. Even if Olivia found a way to free her, Julie would probably cause trouble. But she had to at least try.

"Olivia," Carissa whispered. "Sit by my feet. There's a knife lodged into the side of the sole. See if you can push it out the other side."

"What are you two whispering about?"

"Nothing important. How many captors do we have?" Carissa had to keep Julie talking. At least then she wouldn't hear what Olivia was doing.

"What difference does it make?"

"It matters." Carissa needed to know what she was up against should she ever get free of the infernal ropes.

"I don't see how it will help you, but whatever." Julie hiccupped. "There are four besides me. They're bad news. Don't mess with those guys. Look where it got me."

"How'd you get hooked up with these people?"

"I learned of an opportunity to make a lot of money. I

put feelers out. Personally, I think Kyle turned them on to me. I saw him at the diner at the same time I met them."

Her heart stuttered. Marc had been right. Kyle was a mole. She had to keep Julie talking. Olivia needed more time. She glanced down as the child broke through the last bit of rope. This was perfect. Olivia had freed her legs. The ropes hung loosely in place. She'd only have to kick them away when she was ready. Olivia moved behind her and worked the knife over the ropes. Too bad she hadn't started there first.

"Tell me more about Kyle. How's he figure into this?"

Julie shrugged.

"Why'd you do it, Julie?"

"I told you. For the money." She stood and paced to the window. "This is all your fault. You ruined everything."

Carissa heard voices outside the door and silently willed Olivia to hurry. "Why do you hate me? What did I do to you?"

"It's not about you. This was my big chance to score a ton of money."

"You hurt a little girl. For money? Are you nuts?" Okay maybe that was a bad choice in words, since her friend had clearly lost it.

The door flung open and a masked person stood holding a revolver.

A sharp pain pierced Carissa's wrist. The knife's blade cut deep. Wetness dripped onto her hands.

The masked man waved the gun. "Little girl, get over here."

Olivia hesitated.

He pointed the gun at them. "Now."

Carissa's pulse thrummed in her ears. Helplessness consumed her.

Olivia sobbed. "No. You're a meanie."

His hand tightened on the revolver.

"Sweetie, do what he says." Maybe this would buy her enough time to loosen the ropes the rest of the way and free herself.

Olivia skittered over to the man. He pointed the gun at the child's head.

Carissa closed her eyes. Images of that day so long ago flashed in her mind. Terror filled her. She wasn't enough to save Olivia.

Silent tears slid down the child's face. Carissa closed her eyes, pushing down the horror that consumed her. A verse she'd read not long ago in the book of Matthew popped into her mind "I am with you always." *I need You right now, Lord. Please show me what to do, or send help.*

Marc watched the footage once more. They had to have missed something. There must be a clue.

Frank stood. "Freeze the screen." He peered closer at the image. "See how Julie turns and looks toward the house as though she's startled." He pointed to a shadow on the ground. "Check that out."

"Do you think it's Carissa?"

"Yes. But look here. Run the tape in slow motion."

Carissa's shadow disappeared. "So she walked away."

"No. The image would've changed. Her shadow just disappeared. Why?"

"She fell," Kyle offered.

Frank nodded. "Play the rest."

The tablecloth covered the camera like Kyle had said. Only it didn't blow there naturally. That cloth had been placed over the camera. Kyle should've seen the difference. Marc's pulse tripped. He rounded on Kyle. "You didn't see that?"

A faint flush crept up Kyle's neck. "I must've looked away from the camera for a second. I'm sorry."

Marc balled his fist. This should never have happened.

24

Peace that Carissa couldn't fathom filled her. She focused her gaze on the masked man. "Leave the kid alone. She's worthless to you dead."

He released Olivia and shifted his aim. "If you insist." He approached with his revolver pointed at Carissa's head. Her lips twitched. *Just a little bit closer.* She whipped her leg up kicking the gun from the man's hand. The revolver flew across the room and slid under the bed. "Run, Olivia!"

Carissa broke free of the restraints, stomped on the man's foot, kneed him, then followed with a blow to his nose.

He groaned and dropped to the floor, unconscious.

No time to reach for the weapon. Carissa bolted for the door but skidded to a stop.

Another masked man held Olivia in his grip with a gun to her head.

"Turn around," Olivia's captor said.

Carissa didn't budge. She might be able to take the

man down, but the risk to Olivia was too great. She raised her arms. "Only a coward holds a gun to a child's head. Are you a coward?"

The man's arm lowered slightly then rose again. "Move lady, or I'll kill her."

"I don't think so." Carissa held her breath hoping she hadn't pushed the masked man too far.

His finger flinched.

Silent tears continued to stream down Olivia's face.

"Okay, I'm moving!" She backed into the room with her hands still raised—blood slid down her forearm. She needed to stop the bleeding. The guy she took out still lay sprawled on the floor unconscious. But Julie was gone. How had she sneaked past without being noticed? Curtains on the solitary window blew in the breeze.

"Sit." The man yanked her arm behind her and cursed. "You're bleeding. What a mess." He pulled a hankie from his pocket and pressed it to her wrist then proceeded to tie it, securing it in place. He wrapped the rope around her middle then stepped back and dragged Olivia toward the door. "The kid comes with me."

"No!" Olivia stomped on his foot. He loosened his grip. She tugged away and ran to Carissa. "I want to be with CJ."

"Fine, brat. But you better behave, because if you don't…" He ran his finger across his neck.

Olivia clung to Carissa's hand, which the brainiac had left unbound. These guys may be mean and heartless, but they were definitely amateurs.

"Don't forget your buddy." Carissa nudged the prone man with her tennis shoes.

"He's staying." The masked man walked to the door with the gun still pointed at them.

"Suit yourself." Carissa didn't want the unconscious man in the room. What if he awakened while they were trying to escape?

The door closed firmly, and a lock clicked. Time to get free again and fast. "Are you okay, Olivia?"

The girl nodded, but the crocodile tears in her eyes and her shaking body told a different story.

Carissa understood how she felt. "Come here." She pulled the girl onto her lap. "We're going to escape just like Julie did. We can use this rope to tie up that guy. Can I count on you to stay brave?"

"Yes."

"Good girl."

The tears had slowed and the shakes subsided.

"Okay. Twist the rope around so I can reach the knot from the front."

"It's moving, CJ." Excitement rose in her voice. She tugged the rope until the knot was within easy reach.

"Great work. Now, crawl under the bed and get the gun."

"I'm scared. I can't."

"Yes, you can." Carissa worked the knot while Olivia stood glued to the floor. Another minute, and she'd be free. "Please, sweetie. I need that gun. It'll be okay. Just don't press the trigger."

Olivia hesitated a moment longer before dropping to her hands and knees.

Footsteps outside the door made a tapping sound on the wood floor.

"Quick! Get in my lap."

Olivia jumped up and darted into her lap just as the door opened.

"You have a phone call." The masked man held the receiver to Olivia's ear.

"Hello?"

Carissa could hear the panicked man on the other end. "Are you okay? Did they hurt you?"

"I'm scared, Daddy." Olivia started to cry again.

"That's enough." The thug put the phone to his own ear. "You know what to do." Disconnecting the call, he sneered at them. "Thanks, kid. You just made my boss a very rich man." He cackled and left the room, closing the door and locking it.

"Quick. Get the gun. I'm almost free."

The man on the floor moaned.

Carissa worked the rope faster. One more loop.

The man sat up. "Hey, what's going on?"

Frank hung up the phone with a grim look covering his face. "I've notified the FBI and local authorities."

Marc pocketed his keys. "Okay, let's go."

"Go where?" Frank asked. "We don't have a lead

other than Julie's van. We can't go guns blazing into who knows where."

"But you're a cop." Marc shook his head in disbelief. How could Frank stand there when CJ and Olivia were in trouble?

"No. I *was* a cop. I'm a civilian now, like you."

Kyle excused himself and left the room.

Helpless didn't even begin to describe how Marc felt. He wanted to be out on the front line finding the woman he cared about.

Frank strode to the door. "I need some air."

"Marc, I have something to tell you." Kyle strode into the living room. "But before I do, you have to promise to hear me out."

"I'm listening." Whatever he had to say must be big, because for the first time in a long time, Kyle had that look he got on his face when they were in live combat.

"Shortly after I left the military, I applied to the FBI, and they accepted me. You're my first solo assignment."

"Me? I don't follow." Unease filled him. Why would the FBI be watching him, and why was he Kyle's assignment?

"This project that Olivia's dad is working on is important to the U.S. government. I can't go into detail other than to say you were not given correct information regarding what he's working on. That being said, we needed to make sure Olivia was secure without drawing attention to her location. I was the obvious man for the job. I'm sorry I had to deceive you."

It figures. They were all duped, and a ten-year-old child was paying the price. "So it was all a lie. No one ever came to you saying I owed you money?"

"That was an elaborate story I was forced to perpetuate. I'm sorry. Every time I had to lie to you, it made me sick inside, but someone with a pay grade higher than mine wrote the script, and I had to follow it."

"You were convincing."

"I was trained well. Like I said, I'm sorry. I didn't like lying to you, but I wasn't given a choice. I had to follow orders."

"Was anything you said true? Were your parents killed in a car crash?"

Kyle flinched. "Unfortunately, that is true. I never lied to you about anything that mattered, Marc. I just didn't tell you my real reason for being here. I couldn't. It was a matter of national security."

"But you lied about the guy saying I owed him money." He shot the words out like an arrow. "What about the dude at the aquarium? Who was he?"

"An FBI agent." He shrugged. "Sometimes my job requires things I'm uncomfortable with. I hope you'll forgive me."

Marc heard the contrition in his voice and decided to let the lie slide. He understood duty. "Okay, but why tell me all of this now?"

"I need your help. I messed up earlier. It's my fault that Julie got away with Carissa and Olivia. I still can't figure out how she managed to do it. Carissa could've easily neutralized Julie. Once I confirmed you were all on the up and up and exceptional at your jobs, I was supposed to hang around and offer backup. Theoretically we couldn't fail."

"Yet we did. Now what?"

"We find Olivia."

"And Carissa." No way would Marc allow her to be forgotten in this mess, regardless of the government's interest in Olivia's safe return.

"Right. First things first. I wasn't cleared to fill Frank in, only you."

"Why?"

Kyle shrugged. "Doesn't matter." He went on to explain his plan.

Marc had to admit, Kyle's idea was sound. "Before we do this, I'm curious about something. Did you know Julie was one of them?"

"I suspected, but I had no proof. I observed her while she was at work, talking with the suspects before I made contact with you."

"You mean you were in town doing recon before showing up here?"

He nodded. "I had to know all the players. Julie was the wild card. She had access to the property and was the only one in the equation who didn't benefit from protecting Olivia. I tried to get close to her, but she had eyes for someone else."

"Who?"

"You." He shook his head. "Sometimes you're so blind."

Though generally an alert person, he'd admit to being so into Carissa that he'd barely noticed Julie.

"Come on. We're wasting time."

Carissa stood and the rope fell free. She thrust the man's head down smacking it into the hard floor. "That ought to take care of him."

Olivia handed her the rope. "Do you still need the gun?" Her voice shook.

"Yes, and hurry. As soon as I'm done securing him, we're out of here." She finished tying up the guy but had one last thing to do. Time to see who their captor was. She pulled the mask back and memorized his facial features. Short, dark hair, long artisan nose, pale skin, rounded jaw and defined cheekbones. Too bad she didn't have her phone to take a picture. Her memory would have to suffice.

"Can we go now, CJ?"

"You bet." She reached for the gun and tucked it into her waistband. They ran to the window, and Carissa looked out. They were on the second floor. She swallowed a curse and berated herself for almost returning to her old ways.

"What are we going to do?" Olivia's eyes were wide, and her color had paled.

Good question. If it were just her, she'd jump to the ground like Julie had done, but a ten-year-old girl couldn't jump from a second-story window. She was supposed to protect the kid, not injure her or send her to her death.

Carissa rested her hands on her knees so she was eye level with Olivia. "I need you to trust me."

Olivia nodded.

"Do exactly as I say. I'm going to climb out the window and hang there while you shimmy down my back all the way to my feet. Once you get there I want you to let go."

"No way." She shook her head and stepped away.

Carissa took her by the shoulders. "I know it sounds scary, but it's the best way."

Olivia crossed her arms. "No."

"Do you have a better idea?" She demanded quietly, afraid they'd be heard.

"We could go out the door."

"It's locked, and I'm sure there's someone guarding it. They're not going to leave you in here unrestrained without a guard outside. The window is the only way we're getting out of here." She held her breath. If Olivia refused to cooperate, they were in trouble.

25

Marc's stomach knotted. He didn't like keeping Kyle's information from Frank. Why hadn't the FBI cleared him? Marc needed to know—now. He strode into the bedroom where Kyle had a suitcase filled with an arsenal. "Whoa. Where has that been hiding?"

"The lockbox in the bed of my pickup. You about ready?"

"Almost. I know you don't want to tell me, but I need to know why Frank is out of the loop. I just signed a contract with the man to be his business partner. This is important."

Kyle closed the case and grabbed the handle. "This operation is 'need to know,' and Frank doesn't need to know."

"That's it? There's no dark secret in Frank's past?"

Kyle chuckled. "Not to my knowledge. Frank's a good man. He'll do right by you from what I've been able to find out. He should stick around here with the family in case someone calls with a ransom demand."

Marc raised his brows. "You think they'll call?"

"Hard to say for sure, but my gut says no. If Carissa is half the force I think she is, they won't be able to make that call."

This lightened Marc's mood considerably. Kyle was right. Carissa was amazing at what she did. Frank had shared several stories of their days with the PD. It was why he'd talked her into quitting and joining up with him.

Marc stepped out into the cool dark night, shut the door behind them, then strode beside Kyle. "How long do you think this will take? We should at least tell Frank something."

"Frank's being taken care of, and only God knows when or if we'll find Olivia." Kyle placed the case on the seat between them and slid behind the wheel.

If? He refused to think they wouldn't find the girls. "What do you mean Frank is being taken care of?"

"Don't worry. He's fine. Now let's get a move on. We need to find the kid."

Marc shot an annoyed look at the man he thought he knew and got in beside him. Sure, Olivia was the prize, and he wanted her safe return as much as everyone. But it looked like he was the only one worried about Carissa.

His interest in her had grown since the day they met. He was attracted at first to her light brown hair that glowed when the sun hit it just right and her green eyes, but her sassy, in-your-face attitude mixed with her tender heart for Olivia and her loyalty to her friends is what cinched his feelings. He'd fallen for her, and short of a tsunami, he'd find her. His heart stuttered just thinking about her.

Was she okay? He prayed she was still alive.

"Hey, you with me?" Kyle flicked a glance his way before making a right turn out of the property.

"Yeah, just thinking. I'm worried about Carissa. She can take care of herself, but we both know the only way anyone would've captured her is by impairing her. She wouldn't go without a fight."

"There was no blood in the house. No signs of a struggle." Kyle shrugged. "Don't beat yourself up over this. We suspected they'd make a move to grab Olivia sooner or later. We just made the mistake of assuming they wouldn't strike from the inside."

"Where are we going?"

"Need to know."

"Something tells me by the time this is over, I'm going to hate those three words."

Carissa stared at the closed door. Olivia's life depended on her making the right decision. She had nothing to pick the lock with, and shooting her way out didn't make sense. The door would be hollow and easy to kick through, but it would take time, which they didn't have.

She glanced over her shoulder at the window. Julie

had made it. Surely, they could, too. "I'm sorry, Olivia, but the window is our best option."

Olivia shook her head.

"It'll be okay. We'll pretend it's a game." She could tell from the firm set of the girl's jaw she wouldn't cooperate, and this plan depended fully on Olivia. Carissa strode to the window and peered down into the darkness. The glow from the window was the only light in the back of the house. A small covered area off to the right gave her an idea.

"This is what we're going to do. I'm going to swing you over to a lower roof and from there help you to the ground."

Olivia eyed the distance. "Okay, but don't drop me."

"Sweetie, I have to let go, or you won't get to the second roofline."

Olivia cocked her head to one side. "Are you sure we can't just go out the door?"

"Yes. Now sit on the window ledge." After Olivia was situated, Carissa firmly grasped her wrists. "Okay, slide off the ledge. Don't worry. I won't let go. Once I start to swing, you'll fly a little then drop to the roof. Whatever you do, don't scream. And when you land, bend your legs and roll."

"What if I fall off?"

"You won't." At least she hoped she wouldn't. It was too dark to see the entire rooftop, but the pitch was slight. Olivia would have no problem. Carissa lowered her out the window.

Olivia whimpered.

Carissa swung her to the right. "I'm going to count to three then let go. Remember—stay quiet."

Olivia nodded with her eyes squeezed shut and her lips tucked between her teeth.

Lord, please make this work. "One. Two. Three." She swung Olivia out over the roofline and let go.

The girl yelped, and dropped with a thud to the roof.

Carissa climbed out. Her fingers clung to the windowsill. Pain seared through her wrist so great she almost let go. It still bled from where Olivia had sliced through her skin. She looked down, and her heart stuttered. She couldn't swing over to where Olivia waited. She had to drop.

The bedroom door creaked open. She let go. The earth rushed toward her, and she smacked the solid dirt with both feet. Her knees folded. She rolled several times coming to a stop at the bottom of the sloped yard.

The glow from the window illuminated the backside of the house. Olivia stood. "CJ?" she whispered.

"Shh." She rolled onto all fours then pushed herself to standing, feeling much older than her twenty-nine years.

Crouching low, she raced toward the patio across the grass and held up her arm. "Jump."

Male voices inside the house shouted that they had escaped.

Olivia sprang into her arms.

"Ooph." Air whooshed from her lungs, and they

crumpled to the ground. She released Olivia. "You okay?"

"I think so."

"Good. We need to hurry. Take my hand." They scrambled for the cover of the trees and brush.

Olivia pulled away from her. "You're sticky."

"My wrist is bleeding." The hankie had at least slowed the blood loss.

"Yuck!"

"There's nothing I can do about it right now. We need to get as far from here as possible." She could deal with her wound later. If they stopped now, they'd be caught for sure.

Olivia scuttled beside her as she trudged through the wooded area. Too bad it wasn't a full moon. Then again, if it had been, their captors would be able to see them. The cover of darkness was exactly what they needed.

"CJ, your wrist is bleeding too much."

"It'll be fine." Carissa brushed off Olivia's concern even though she was lightheaded and feared she may be bleeding more than she'd realized. Surely, Olivia hadn't nicked a major artery, or she'd be dead by now.

Marc peered into the darkness as they passed familiar landmarks. "It might be helpful if I knew where we're going."

"Doubtful, just keep your eyes open."

"What am I looking for?"

"Julie's catering van. Anything suspicious."

Marc suddenly realized the bleakness of their situation. Without any leads, they were driving aimlessly in the hope of stumbling upon Carissa and Olivia. Surely, the FBI had an idea of where they were.

"You mentioned doing recon before you joined up with me. Did you happen to find out where the suspects were staying?"

"Of course. The place was raided almost immediately, but it was abandoned."

Helplessness settled around Marc. Would he ever see Carissa again?

"I know it doesn't look good right now, but there're things you don't know—can't know." His cell played the theme song from *Rocky*.

"Seriously?"

Kyle ignored him and took the call.

Marc listened intently to the one-way conversation.

"Got it. And thanks." He disconnected the cell and punched the accelerator.

Carissa stumbled and fell to her knees. "Maybe you're right, Olivia. I need to stop this bleeding." The hankie had fallen off at some point—the dude seriously had no clue how to tie a knot. She wore a cami under her top.

If she could tear off a good-sized portion and tie it around her wrist to stop the blood. She reached under her shirt and grasped the cotton fabric and tugged—nothing. She felt for the seam and tried again. The ripping sounded like a thunder cloud in the quiet of the woods, but she managed to tear off a sizable piece.

Carissa applied pressure to the wound with the fabric.

"What are we going to do, CJ?"

Good question. She had no idea where they were or which direction to go. But lightheaded or not, they had to keep moving. Beams from flashlights lit an area not far from the house. "We need to move. Stay close."

Olivia fisted the hem of Carissa's shirt, and they moved deeper into the brush. A twig snapped under her foot. She froze and listened—silence, then shouts. Time to run.

"Hang on tight. We need to get out of here." Carissa switched directions, hoping to throw their captors off the trail. Then the earth gave way. She reached for something—anything to grab onto but found nothing except weeds and weak plants that uprooted in her hand. The ground rushed past, she twisted her ankle, lost footing, then slid to her bottom.

Carissa barely noticed Olivia clinging to her as they continued to slide further down a deep ravine. She gave up trying to stop their plunge and wrapped her good arm around the child hoping to shield her from much of the debris that now slapped her face. They smacked into something hard, stopping their decent. Her ankle throbbed. But that was the least of her problems. Reaching out in the darkness, she felt a huge tree trunk.

Carissa sat up, held Olivia at arm's length and whispered. "Are you hurt?"

"Not too bad. I don't think anything's broken."

She pulled the girl into a tight hug. "Thank God."

"Where are we?"

"I have no idea. But we're probably safe for now. We'll stay put until daylight and then hike out of here."

"What about the bad guys?"

"I don't think they'd follow us down here. We must've fallen fifty feet or more. We're fine for the time being."

"I hope you're right."

The ground shook beneath them, and the woods seemed to come alive. Something big was racing toward them.

"What's that?" Olivia cried.

26

Marc straightened in his seat when Kyle turned down a dirt road. "Where're we going?"

"Just wait." Tension tightened Kyle's voice.

"I don't want to wait." Marc snapped. "After all the secrets you've kept from me, I think you owe me a straight answer. What was that phone call about?"

Kyle braked hard and rounded a corner. "Let's get one thing straight," he said, his tone firm. "I don't owe you anything. I'm doing my job the best I know how. If you don't like that I kept things from you—too bad." He pressed the accelerator hard, and they surged forward. "We don't have much time. Stay alert."

If Carissa's life was not depending on them right now, he'd let Kyle have it, but as it stood, he needed Kyle and his expertise. He looked out the front window searching for anything that would lead him to her.

Kyle slowed, pulled off to the side, and killed the engine. "We hike from here." He reached for the door handle.

Marc held his place. "Hold on. We need a plan, and I want to know what's going on."

Kyle sighed and faced him. "The police received a tip from a neighbor about unusual activity at a vacation house up the road. They passed the info on to us. We're following up."

"Thank you. You think this is where the girls are being held?" His heart rate tripped into double time. The place was out of the way and a good distance from town. The landscape consisted mostly of tall fir trees and underbrush, great stomping grounds for wild animals. He'd heard a cougar had been spotted up this way not too long ago. Good thing they were armed.

"That's what we're here to find out. If it's them, we'll wait for backup. If not, we move on." Kyle grabbed a black backpack.

"What's in there?"

"Supplies. I like to be prepared." He got out and slipped it on. Then he grabbed the arsenal bag.

At least one of them was prepared. Marc opened the door and stepped out. The sooner they got to this house the better. One thing bothered him though. They were only two men up against who knew how many. He didn't like that one bit. They raced to the edge of the yard and held their position. The lights inside were on, and men were shouting. Marc inched beside Kyle and pointed to a man who passed by an exposed window. "He has a gun."

Kyle pulled his cell out and sent a text.

"Now what?"

"We wait for backup."

"What if they get away?"

Kyle hunkered down and yanked Marc alongside him. "We don't even know if those are our guys. It's not against the law to carry a gun."

"But you think it's them, or you wouldn't have sent for backup. What if the backup is too late? We could at least sneak up to a window and see if the girls are inside."

"We're waiting for backup. We won't do Olivia any good if we're caught."

"Or Carissa," Marc muttered under his breath. He had to find her and fast. The longer she went missing the greater the chance they wouldn't find her alive.

Carissa pulled Olivia close and pressed up against the large fir. Whatever was headed their direction sounded like a stampede. The sound grew louder. Her pulse ran wild. What had they awakened?

Out of the darkness, large dark shapes appeared and drew closer. Then she saw them. A herd of elk galloped in their direction, kicking up dirt and muck in their wake. The elk rushed past then disappeared into the dark. Stillness surrounded them.

Carissa spoke into Olivia's ear. "We must've disturbed their sleep when we slid down the hillside."

"Wow." Olivia let the word trail off into a whisper.

"Oh yeah." A few minutes later, Carissa's pulse slowed, and she relaxed into the rough surface of the tree, closing her eyes. The hopelessness of their situation weighed heavily. They were God knows where, injured, and tired, without food, shelter, or means to find their way out of the mess they were in.

"CJ?"

"Hmm?"

"I'm cold."

Carissa pulled Olivia close and held her tight. "Me, too. We'll keep each other warm."

A shudder passed through Olivia before she relaxed and rested her head against Carissa's shoulder. Minutes later, the soft rhythmic breathing of the sleeping child gave her a moment of satisfaction. At least one of them would get a little shuteye, but for Carissa's part, she had a job to do—keep Olivia out of the hands of the enemy and find their way back to civilization. The problem was, she couldn't do it alone.

For the first time in her life since she'd vowed to protect those around her, she was at a loss. She tried to move her ankle and winced. Promising Olivia they'd hike out at first light was probably a mistake. Her ankle was as swollen as a water balloon.

"I don't like the look of this." Marc peered through

brush toward the lit house. "What do you think is going on?"

"Beats me." Kyle opened his pack and pulled out binoculars. "I see two men. Both armed and agitated."

"Any sign of the girls?"

"No. Let's move. Maybe there are windows in back." Kyle crouched and scurried along the perimeter of the yard.

Marc hung close behind, staying alert for trouble. If this was the right place, wouldn't they be able to see them through one of the windows? But whatever was going on inside, it didn't look right. Something was definitely going down.

Kyle stopped and crouched beside a large alder. "I recognize that man." He handed the binoculars to Marc.

"Who is he?"

"He approached Julie the day I had her under surveillance."

Marc knew that meant they'd found the house. Hope surged. They needed to overtake the place before anyone inside knew what was going on. It was only a matter of time until he could hold Carissa again. "How long until backup arrives?"

"I'm guessing five minutes or less. They'll hike in like we did."

Adrenaline pumped through Marc's veins. He wanted to storm the house but thought better of it. Footsteps crunched through the dry earth behind them.

Kyle motioned for him to hide. He crouched low

beside a bush and held his breath. It was probably the team they were waiting for, but something about Kyle's attitude had him on edge.

A man ran into the clearing then through the yard and into the house. Loud shouting emerged through an open window.

"I wonder what that's all about," Kyle whispered before he crept closer to the house and motioned for Marc to stay put.

Marc kept a lookout for trouble. If Kyle was spotted, then they were done for. He jumped when the barrel of a gun dug into his back.

"Put your hands where I can see them," someone demanded.

Marc raised his arms.

The man pilfered Marc's wallet. "Okay, you can relax. Sorry about that, Marc. We didn't know if you were one of them or not."

Marc turned. A man clothed in black with black war paint on his white skin peered back at him. "You're our backup, I presume."

"Yep. What's the situation?"

Kyle had crept over and spoke up explaining the situation to the SWAT team.

The team leader devised a plan, which didn't include either of them. Marc wasn't happy. He wanted to be in there when they found Carissa and Olivia. But these guys were trained for this kind of thing, so he conceded.

The team got into place, leaving Marc and Kyle to watch the invasion from a laptop someone had thrust into his hands.

He heard shouting and saw the team storm the house. A large man ran from the room, and the camera followed. Seconds later, a SWAT member had him pinned to the floor and cuffed. More shouting and then quiet. A few minutes later, the leader approached them. "This is the place, but the girls aren't here. We weren't able to get much info yet, but it seems the kid and her bodyguard escaped about an hour ago. We'll run these guys in and see what more we can find out."

Okay, not the news he'd hoped to hear, but it didn't surprise him either. "What do we do now?" Marc looked over his shoulder into the woods, and his stomach dropped. The property stretched for miles. They could be out here for days and not find them, especially if Carissa was trying to not be found.

"Olivia wake up." Carissa shifted the child in her arms. Sunrays filtered through the trees, causing dancing light to hit the ground around them.

Olivia stirred and opened her eyes slowly. She stretched and stood.

Carissa rolled over onto all fours and tried to push up. Pain sliced up her arm and leg. She caught her breath, dug deep, and hauled herself up. The world tilted, and she reached out for the tree.

"CJ!" Olivia grabbed her around the waist.

"Thanks. I'll be okay in a second." At least she hoped so. The cut on her wrist had stopped bleeding, but in its place was an inflamed wound. She tried putting pressure on her swollen ankle—not good. "Olivia, I need a walking stick. Do you think you could find something lying nearby that will work?"

"I'll try."

Fear rattled in the girl's voice.

"When we get home, I'm going to make us the biggest hot fudge sundaes ever," Carissa said in a cheerful voice.

"With whipped cream and a cherry?"

"You bet." She smiled. "How's the search going?"

Olivia held up a long thick stick that stretched above her head. "How about this?"

"Perfect!" She held out her hand. "You ready to get out of here?"

"Oh yeah." Olivia took her free hand and looked up at her face. A smudge of dirt covered her nose and dust had settled on her cheeks.

Under any other circumstance, Carissa would find the kid's appearance cute.

"Do you know the way home?" Olivia asked.

"Not exactly." Carissa took a step and nearly buckled to the ground. Her eyes burned from unshed tears.

"CJ, you're hurt. Maybe we should stay here until someone finds us."

"Except the people looking for us are the bad guys."

Olivia's lip puckered.

"Don't worry. I'll think of something."

Olivia dropped her hand and skirted around the tree. "I see something down there. It looks like a barn." She came back around Carissa. "I could go and get help. It's not that far."

"No way. You're my responsibility. We stick together."

Olivia chewed her lip for a moment then her eyes brightened. "It's all downhill. We can slide on our bottoms like we did last night."

Other than the risk of catching her foot on something and damaging it even worse, Carissa liked the idea and honestly had nothing better to suggest. "Okay. We're probably covered in so much dirt and mud by now we'll blend right in, and no one will even notice us." Carissa hopped on one foot to the opposite side of the tree that had stopped their decent last night and sucked in her breath. "Whoa." They were standing on a shelf of sorts and the slope beneath was steep. No way could she climb down standing. Sliding was her only option and the safest choice for Olivia, too.

Olivia sat like she was about to go down a slide. She patted the earth next to her. "Come on, CJ. Don't we need to hurry in case the bad guys figure out we're here?"

Carissa plopped down. "Here goes nothing." She

grasped Olivia's hand with her good one.

Olivia nodded and pushed off.

Carissa followed, feeling every bump in the uneven earth. *Ooph.* Something scraped her leg, and she heard a rip. Olivia seemed to be faring better, even giggling as she slid down the hillside, but Carissa found nothing delightful about the bone-jarring ride. The slope evened out, and they slowed to a stop.

"That was fun!" Olivia stood and brushed her hands against her jeans. "Look. There's the barn I saw."

Carissa stood and moaned. "I left the walking stick at the top."

"That's okay. I'll help you."

"Thanks, but maybe I should hop. We'll go faster that way. I don't want to be out in the open if the bad guys come looking for us here." Speaking of which…a man wearing jeans and a denim jacket emerged from the building in question. Was that a gun in his hand?

27

Marc grabbed a daypack and slipped it on. Sunshine barely lit the new day. One way or another, they'd find Carissa, but the blood they'd found where she was being held worried him. What if they were too late?

The lowlifes had sung like canaries in interrogation and pegged Julie as their inside source. She'd played them all for fools. He wanted to find her almost as much as Carissa, but for vastly different reasons. Traitors like Julie made him sick.

Kyle strode toward him. "They found two sets of footprints leading into the woods. We'll follow the prints, and if we're lucky, they'll lead us right to the girls. Stop worrying, Marc. This is almost over, and now that we have custody of the group who threatened her, Olivia will be able to go home soon."

"You sure about that? I doubt they had their entire organization situated here."

"Agreed."

Marc walked beside Kyle through the woods about twenty feet. Then the trail disappeared.

"Looks like we might need to call in the dogs." Kyle pulled out his phone and sent a text. "Olivia's dad is set to deliver his finished product any day."

"So the kid's still in danger. I wish her dad would work faster." They continued to walk in the general direction they'd been going, traversing through scattered brush and tall fir trees.

"The immediate threat has been removed. I seriously doubt they'll go after Olivia again. We've put a nice kink in their organization."

"I hope you're right, but just in case, don't you think we should take her to a safehouse?"

Kyle grinned. "Your talent is being wasted being a bodyguard. You should apply with the FBI." He looked around as if they weren't alone and lowered his voice. "I'm not supposed to tell you this, but as soon as we find Olivia, a safehouse will be the first order of business. However, your services will no longer be needed."

"I think I liked your 'need to know' replies better. What can I do to convince you to let my team stay on her detail?"

"It's not me you need to convince. It's the way things work. Sorry." He pointed to one of the many wild rhododendrons. "That bush looks like someone barreled into it."

They passed by the rhododendron and spotted footprints beyond the damaged bush that led to a drop off.

Marc's stomach lurched. "Do you think…?"

"Looks like they went over." Kyle waved his arm across the expanse.

"I don't see them."

"Me neither. You want to head down or wait for the dogs?" Kyle asked.

"Let's move on. Is there someone waiting at the house for the dog?"

"Yes. An agent went to the estate to pick up clothing belonging to the girls. The dog will get their scent and go from there with its handler."

"With any luck we'll find them first. I hate that they spent the night out here."

"Yeah." Kyle's voice was soft. "You ready? It's pretty steep."

"Let's do this."

"CJ, I know this place." Olivia's face lit with excitement.

"Shh. We don't want to give ourselves away."

"But it's okay. We've been here before." Olivia pulled her forward.

Carissa hobbled, gingerly putting pressure on her bum ankle.

"See that trail over there and that shed? This is where we went riding. That must be the backside of the horse barn."

Hope surged through Carissa. "You're right. But the man has a gun."

Olivia yanked her arm. "There he is again. I don't think that's a gun. It's a tool."

Carissa looked closer. "It's a drill." A giggle bubbled up, and Carissa couldn't suppress it. "Boy, do I need a vacation."

"Or glasses." Olivia smirked.

She gave the girl a quick hug and took her hand. "Come on."

The same man they'd seen before crossed the yard, seemingly unaware of their presence. Uncertainty stopped Carissa. Could she trust him?

Olivia pulled on her hand. "Let's go. I'm sure he'll help us."

"Do you recognize him from when we went riding?"

"No, but we didn't see everyone that works here. Grandpa says they have part-time workers in exchange for boarding their horse."

"Oh. That makes sense." She shook off dizziness and took a step forward. Her leg gave way, and she cried out, hitting the earth with a smack.

"CJ!" Olivia knelt over her. "I'll get help." She stood and bolted.

"No! Wait." Too late. *Lord, please keep Olivia safe.* Peace settled over Carissa, and clarity hit her like a crashing wave. She wasn't God, and she couldn't always be there. He had everything under control. Sure, bad stuff happened, but each and every time she'd failed, He'd shone. He brought them out of the darkness into the safety of the familiar. No matter how hard she tried to protect everyone around her, she was fallible, but God wasn't. She'd trusted the wrong person, but God didn't make mistakes. No, He knew exactly where they needed to go for help.

Olivia ran toward her with the cowboy in the lead. She stopped and dropped down beside her. "He called 9-1-1. Everything will be okay, CJ."

Carissa grinned. "You did good."

The man cleared his throat. "You must be, CJ. I'm Rex." He held out his hand. "I hear you and your little friend ran into some trouble."

"You could say that. May I use your phone? There are a few people who will be relieved to know we're safe."

"You bet we are."

Carissa started at the familiar male voice. She turned. "Marc!" Her eyes locked on his face. "You found us." The joy and love in his eyes made her heart trip.

"Of course we did." He squatted beside her, and everyone else faded. Ever so slowly, he brushed her hair behind her ears then cupped her face in his hands. "I've never been so happy to see someone. Are you okay?"

She held her breath and nodded.

He leaned toward her and captured her lips with his. Her body warmed as she returned his kiss.

One of the men cleared his throat.

Marc drew back. "Promise me you'll never let anyone grab you again."

She grinned. "I'll do my best. Have you found Julie?"

"We've been focused on finding you and Olivia."

Kyle squatted beside them. "I'm glad to see you're okay, but we need to move Olivia to a safehouse."

Hands on her hips, Olivia glared at Kyle. "CJ's hurt. I think she broke her ankle, and her wrist is cut bad. It bled a lot."

Kyle raised his hands. "Calm down. We'll make sure she gets the medical attention she needs, but in the meantime, you need to come with me to a safe place."

Olivia stomped her foot. "I'm not leaving CJ."

"I thought you said you were okay," Marc whispered in her ear.

She shrugged.

Kyle rubbed his chin "I guess she'll have to come with us."

Relief washed over Carissa. For a moment, she thought she'd never see the kid again, and she wasn't ready to say good-bye.

"I have her." Marc scooped Carissa into his arms.

"Put me down," she said, but her heart shouted that he should never let her go. She almost giggled at her sappy thoughts. This was not like her. It must be the lack of sleep.

"Nope." Marc winked at Kyle. "Whose arm do you have to twist to keep us all together?"

Kyle sighed and pulled out his cell.

"What are you talking about, Marc?"

"I'll explain everything later. Let's just say that there's more to Kyle than we realized."

"Seems to me you folks could use a lift." The cowboy gestured toward a crew cab pickup.

"Sorry for ignoring you, Rex," Carissa said.

"Not at all. I'd be happy to drop you wherever you need to go."

Kyle pocketed his phone. "That won't be necessary. There's a car en route to get us."

Carissa rested her head on Marc's shoulder in no hurry to go anywhere.

The next day Carissa tried to focus on Frank, but all she could think about was how Olivia had been whisked away to a safehouse. The girl had wanted Carissa to stay with her, but in the end the FBI won, and they were cut out.

"When I get my hands on Marc..."

"This isn't like you, Frank. Why are you so angry?"

"He's our partner, and he went rogue." He paced the living space in the guesthouse that they would soon vacate.

Carissa closed her eyes against the dizzying effect of Frank circling. She'd hoped to calm her friend before Marc arrived, but at this rate, her goal didn't look promising. "He didn't go rogue. He did what he thought was best for our client. He showed initiative."

"How was cutting me out in our client's best interest?"

Carissa shrugged. "I don't think he was given an option, Frank. Please be reasonable."

The door opened, and Marc strode in. He took one look at Frank and froze. "I know you're angry, Frank."

"You're right about that. How could you?"

"I had no choice. I either went along with the FBI or got cut out. I had to make a quick decision. I did what I thought was best."

Marc walked deeper into the space and sat on the arm of the chair Carissa occupied. "Hey there," he said softly. He gently squeezed her shoulder and then turned to Frank. "Please try to see things from my perspective. I wanted to talk to you and fill you in before we left, but Kyle wouldn't let me. He said we needed to move and that you were being taken care of. I had no idea what that meant, but I trusted him."

Frank stopped pacing, sighed, and plopped into the nearest chair. "Fine."

"Fine?" Marc raised a brow. "Does this mean we're good?"

"Yes. But don't ever let the FBI railroad you again."

Carissa covered her mouth to hide a smile.

"What're you smiling about?" Frank snapped then winked and tossed a throw pillow at her.

"Hey, watch the leg." Her ankle, though not broken, had a bad sprain and was very tender.

Marc laced his fingers through hers and gently

254

stroked the bandage covering her wrist, which had seven stitches. "I'm confused about this meeting. I thought since Olivia was under FBI protection we were done."

Carissa's shoulder's tightened. "I still feel bad about leaving her alone like that."

"There was nothing you could do." Frank propped an ankle on his knee. "Besides, her grandparents are with her."

"I know. But we went through so much together."

"One thing still eats at me," Marc said. "Julie's out there. I won't be able to rest until that woman's behind bars."

"Don't worry. She'll turn up sooner or later." Carissa had no doubt justice would be served where Julie was concerned. "In the meantime, let's focus on getting back to Seattle and starting our next job."

Frank cleared his throat. "I blocked out the next two weeks. We've been working hard all summer and could use a break."

"What am I supposed to do for two weeks?" Carissa couldn't be idle that long. Then again, she really could use a vacation.

"Beats me. You might try recuperating from your injuries." Frank stood. "My bags and your espresso machine are in my car. See you at the office in two weeks. I'm going fishing." He casually saluted them both then left.

Marc moved to the chair Frank vacated. "I don't

have plans either. Maybe we could spend some time getting to know one another better."

"I'd like that. My ride back to Seattle just left. Can I bum one with you?"

He grinned. "No problem. It'll give us time to talk."

"It's funny. I feel as if I've known you forever after all we've gone through this past summer." She pushed up. No way would she sit around recuperating like Frank suggested. "But maybe we could find Julie before we leave town."

Marc jumped up and reached out to support her.

"I'm fine, Marc. Don't baby me." She softened her words with a smile. "Please."

He pulled his hand back and frowned. "How are we going to do what the police and the FBI haven't been able to accomplish?"

"Simple. I know Julie." At least she had. She grabbed her purse and limped to the door. "You coming?"

28

"Where to?" Marc started the engine of his pickup. Julie had cost them all enough, and if Carissa thought she could locate the woman, then he'd be by her side to make sure Julie didn't get away.

Carissa's phone buzzed. He listened in on the one-sided conversation.

"No. When? Where? Marc and I'll help in any way we can. Okay, bye."

"What was that about?"

"That was Linda. Olivia slipped out unnoticed. The FBI thought she might have come here."

Fear for Olivia sliced through him. "She ran from the feds?"

"It appears so. She pretended to be taking a nap and snuck out the window in her bedroom." She shook her head and jutted out her jaw. "I can't believe she did that. She was terrified to escape through the window in the room where we were held."

"Sounds like she overcame her fear."

"She's going to get herself killed." Her voice caught.

Marc reached out and took her hand. "We'll find her."

"How?" Carissa turned to him with glistening eyes.

"She couldn't have gone far on foot."

Carissa shook her head. "They think she took a horse from a nearby stable. The owner reported a missing mare around the same time Olivia disappeared."

"How did she get away? Didn't they have anyone posted in the driveway?" Frustration didn't begin to describe his feelings. "Where's this stable?"

She rattled off the address that Linda had given her.

Marc entered the address into his phone and studied the map for a moment. "I know where she went." A short time later, he pulled into the driveway of the place where they'd found Carissa and Olivia. For the most part, the place looked deserted except for a few cars and a truck with a flatbed trailer attached.

"You really think this is where she came?"

"Yes. She knows this place, and it's close to the safehouse." Marc parked and shifted to face her. "What do we do now?"

"I suppose we could ask the owners about borrowing a couple horses."

"One will be plenty. You're in no condition to be riding solo." Besides, he'd enjoy having her arms wrapped around his waist.

"You're probably right." She rubbed the bandage on her wrist.

"Are the stitches bothering you?"

"A little, but I think it's mostly the tape that's aggravating my raw skin." She reached for the door handle. "We might run into a little resistance if the FBI is still around. Linda said everyone was pretty uptight."

"Yeah, well they ought to be. How could they lose a ten-year-old girl in protective custody?"

"Just like we did. Linda said Olivia was bored and had been asking to go riding. They told her no." Carissa shrugged. "You know what she's like."

"I sure do. But if she only wanted to go riding, why hasn't she returned?"

"Good question." Carissa opened the door and stepped out.

Marc ran around to the passenger side and offered his arm. Since she refused to use crutches the hospital sent home with her, she could at least lean on him.

Someone stepped out of the house and waved.

Marc let go of Carissa. "Wait here. I'll be right back." He strode toward the woman. "Hi. I'm Marc Olsen. We're friends of the girl that's suspected of stealing your horse."

The woman frowned and crossed her arms. "The FBI was already here. They're out on ATVs looking for her right now." That explained the pickup and trailer he'd spotted.

"I see. Carissa Jones and I were in charge of Olivia's protection for most of the summer, and we grew attached to her."

The woman's face softened. "Such a shame a child needs protecting like that. I've known Linda and Roger for years, and I just can't fathom all of this. It's crazy."

"I agree. We were wondering if you'd allow us to borrow one of your horses. We'd like to help in the search."

"I suppose that would be all right. I presume you know how to ride."

"Yes, ma'am. I grew up in the saddle."

The woman chuckled. "Sounds like my own childhood." She nodded toward Carissa. "What about her? She ride? I have several gentle horses if she needs one."

"Thanks for the offer, but Carissa was injured recently and would be safer riding double with me if that's okay with you."

"Sure. Poor thing. I still can't believe all that's happened, and so close to my property, too. Makes me want to sell and move further from town." She sighed. "But that'd kill business."

Marc wanted to be polite but also sensed Carissa's growing impatience even from twenty feet away. "I'm sure it would. If you don't mind, I'll go saddle up a horse."

"Of course. I'll show you where everything is."

Carissa stepped onto the ladder the woman provided and

swung up behind Marc. The horse shifted, and she flung her arms around his waist in a death grip.

He chuckled and patted her hands. "Relax. If you squeeze the life out of me, we won't get very far."

Carissa loosened her hold. "Sorry." Her face heated, and she was glad he didn't have eyes in the back of his head. After thanking the horse's owner, they rode along the same trail Olivia had used the last time they went riding. She wanted to rest her head against his back, but she needed to stay alert. They were there for one reason, to find Olivia and return her to safety.

"You see anything?"

"Not yet."

"Don't you think the FBI would've found her by now?" Marc's voice held concern.

She didn't answer because his thoughts echoed her own. If Olivia was on the property, she'd be easy to find. The agents had at least thirty minutes on them, plus they could split up and check the various trails. Unless Olivia had been thrown again and was lying in the bushes injured and out of sight. In that case, finding her would be more difficult. But her horse should still be easy to spot. Her stomach churned. "I wonder how long Olivia was missing before anyone realized it?"

"Why?"

"Just a hunch. Let's head back to the barn."

"We haven't gone very far. There are still miles of trails to search."

"I know, but if I'm right, we're wasting our time."

"And if you're wrong?"

"Please, Marc. Humor me."

He patted her hand and turned the horse around. "I hope you're right."

"Me, too." In spite of the tense situation, peace flowed through her. Her shoulders relaxed, and she leaned a little closer to Marc. A smile even teased her lips. "When this is all over, I think you should ask me out."

Marc glanced over his shoulder. "You got it." He urged the horse into a trot.

"Whoa. Take it easy. I'm going to bounce off."

"Sorry. I was thinking about that date."

Carissa would've slugged him in the shoulder except she feared falling. The barn came into view, and they rode up to the door. Nothing had changed since they'd left. Marc held Carissa's arm as she slid off.

He swung down and offered his arm, which she gratefully took.

"Do you care to share what you're thinking?"

She shook her head, touched her finger to her lips, then opened the door and stepped inside. After letting her eyes adjust to the dim light, she raised her voice. "I can't imagine where Olivia would've gone. I thought she loved her parents and wanted to go home to them, but I guess I was wrong. Seems like she wants to live the life of an orphan and never see her parents or friends again."

Questions filled Marc's eyes. "Ah...yeah. I suppose

you're right. I really thought Olivia loved her family. Guess I was wrong."

"Seems to me she'd have to hate her family to do this to them."

"I do not!" Olivia, holding a kitten, popped out from behind a stack of hay.

Carissa did her best to keep a stern face. "You sure don't act like it. Why'd you run off and hide?"

Olivia dragged her hand along the kitten's back and walked toward them. "They wouldn't let me go outside. I wanted to see if the kittens had been born."

"Why's there a loose horse?" Carissa asked.

Olivia ducked her chin. "I thought about trying to ride again, but got scared. The horse pulled away from me and ran off." She held the snow-white kitten up to Carissa. "Isn't she beautiful?"

"Yes, she is." Carissa petted the feline. "Any idea where the horse went?"

Olivia's eyes pooled. "I don't know. I've been in here."

"But you had to know people were looking for you." Irritation laced Marc's voice. "Didn't you hear us in here earlier saddling a horse?"

"Yes, but I was playing with the kittens. I didn't want to be found yet, so I hid." She set the kitten on the floor and looked up at them. "I suppose you're going to make me go back now."

"You got it." Carissa pulled out her phone. "How about you give your grandma a call?"

Olivia took the device. "Okay." She started to press in the number and stopped. "Is she angry?"

"Guess you'll have to call her to find out." Carissa didn't feel too sorry for the kid. Olivia knew better than to run off and deserved whatever punishment she got, but at the same time, she empathized with her. No one enjoyed being caged up.

Olivia handed her the phone back. "Thanks. Grandma said to stay put, and one of the agents will be here soon to take me back."

Carissa wanted to help Olivia feel safe and content again and then it hit her. "Olivia, do you remember my wishing quilt?"

"Yes."

"I think you need one too. I'll keep an eye out for one I think you'd like and mail it to you when I find one."

"Really?" Her voice held awe. "You'd do that for me? Even after all the trouble I caused?"

Carissa glanced at Marc and saw his brows rise. "Yes. What do you say? Would you like your own quilt?"

"Oh yes, please. I'll take very good care it."

"I'm sure you will. But you have to make me a promise." The sound of several ATV engines roared close by and then stopped.

Olivia nodded.

"No more running away. And if you need someone to talk to, you can always call me."

"I promise."

"Good. I'll make sure you get a blanket, but right now, Marc and I need to find Julie."

Kyle stepped into the barn. "Hey, everyone." He walked to Olivia and placed a hand on her shoulder. "Looks like you found our runaway—again."

"Seems that way." Marc handed him the horse's reins. "Think you can take care of this?" He wrapped Carissa's arm through his and without a backward glance guided her from the barn.

Carissa chuckled. "That was mean."

Marc shrugged. "Don't spoil my fun. Did you see the look on his face?"

"Mm-hmm. Priceless."

29

"Stop." Carissa craned her neck toward a glimmer of metal she'd spotted in the brush off the highway on their way back to town.

"What? Why?"

"I thought I saw a car back there."

He kept driving. "We need to find Julie, not investigate random cars."

"People have been known to crash around here and not be found for days or weeks. I thought I saw some metal shimmering in the brush back there. I want to check it out."

"Oh. Okay." Marc slowed his pickup and made a U-turn.

"Pull over here." Carissa hopped out and limped along the side of the road. She'd only gone ten feet or so when Marc came up beside her.

She turned to him. "We need to cross. I think it's right around here." They hustled across the highway together, and she sucked in her breath. "Look, skid marks." Someone had definitely lost control. She followed the marks to where they met gravel and then dirt. Tire tracks led into the brush, and sure enough, the back bumper of a van. The van sat crumpled against a huge fir tree.

Marc plowed ahead of her.

Carissa scrambled after him. "Is there anyone inside?"

His face paled. "Yes. Julie."

"Oh no." She rushed forward. "Is she…?" She couldn't finish the question. Instead she pulled out her cell and called 9-1-1.

Marc opened the door, reached inside, and felt for a pulse. A moment later, he closed it and shook his head. "I'm sorry, but we're too late."

Carissa's legs turned to jelly. Even after all the hurt Julie had caused, she didn't wish her friend dead. Her throat thickened with tears.

Marc wrapped his arm around her shoulder. "Come on. Let's wait up by the road." He held her close and guided them out of the brush. "I'm so sorry, Carissa. I wanted to see justice done but not this."

"I know." She buried her face in his chest and silent tears poured down her cheeks and onto her chin wetting the front of Marc's shirt.

Marc held her, his strong arms exactly what she needed.

A few minutes later, Carissa wiped her face on her arm and stepped back from him. "I know she was horrible, but she wasn't always like that." Sirens blared in the distance. "How's my face?"

He gently rubbed her cheek with his thumb. "Better."

A police cruiser pulled up. She recognized the cop from the day Olivia had run away at the ice cream shop. She wiped her eyes with her fingers the best she could and then took a deep breath, letting it out slowly while Marc explained the situation to the officer.

"I suppose someone should notify the FBI, too." Marc pulled out his phone. "I'll call Kyle."

Carissa watched the scene unfold around her and though she was sad for the loss of her friend, she was relieved to have everything wrapped up. Olivia would be going home by the end of the week, and they had the next two weeks wide open.

Marc took her hand and led her back to his pickup. "I think it's time you and I followed orders."

"What'd you have in mind?"

The twinkle in his eyes held a promise—one she aimed to take hold of and never let go.

Epilogue

Carissa along with Marc and Frank sat around the conference room table at their office in Seattle. The past two weeks had been idyllic. She and Marc had taken their time driving back to Seattle and had spent countless hours together, but it was time to get back to real life now. She looked forward to diving into another job. "I heard from Linda Drummond this morning."

Frank's eyes widened. "Everything okay?"

"Yes. Olivia is settled back with her parents at their home in Phoenix. She's telling all her friends about the great summer she had hanging out at the beach in Oregon."

Marc chuckled. "Now she had fun."

Carissa grinned. "She is a little drama queen."

"Makes life more interesting." Frank clicked the mouse on his computer and the screen on the wall lit up with the photo of a young woman. "Are the two of you ready to move on to our next client?"

"Absolutely." She couldn't wait to get back to work.

She reached under the table and grasped Marc's hand.

Her gaze locked with his. A soft smile lit his face.

Frank groaned. "Is this what I have to look forward to from the two of you?"

"It's all your fault," Carissa said. "If you hadn't hired Marc behind my back…"

Frank raised his hands in surrender. "I see I only have myself to blame." The smile on his face belied his pleasure that they were an official couple. "Now, focus or I'm going to have to separate the two of you. He winked then clicked his mouse again. "Word about Protection Inc. has spread, and we have several people requesting our services. We work well as a team, but I think it's time to bring in some staff."

Carissa nodded. Anticipation for the potential of their company and their future filled her with joy she hadn't experienced since she was a child. She squeezed Marc's hand and returned her attention to the screen. Time to work.

Coming soon *Imminent Threat*, book two in the
Protection Inc. series.

Author Note

Dear Reader,

Lincoln City is a town I've enjoyed visiting since I was a young teen. My husband and I actually went there for our honeymoon nearly thirty years ago.

If you enjoyed *Direct Threat*, please consider posting a review on Amazon.

Watch for *Imminent Threat* to release soon.

Author Acknowledgement

I would like to acknowledge all of the people who had a hand in the making of this book: proofreaders, my editor, my critique group, beta readers, and my law enforcement contact. Special thanks to all of you! I couldn't have done this without you.

Blessings,
Kimberly Rose Johnson

More Books by Kimberly Rose Johnson

Protection Inc.
Imminent Threat

Law Enforcement Heroes
Edge of Truth

The Librarian Sleuth
The Sleuth's Miscalculation
The Sleuth's Dilemma
The Sleuth's Conundrum
The Sleuth's Surprise (October 2020)

Brides of Seattle
Until I Met You
The Reluctant Groom
Simply Smitten

Melodies of Love
A Love Song for Kayla
An Encore for Estelle
A Waltz for Amber

Sunriver Dreams
A Love to Treasure
A Christmas Homecoming
Designing Love

Wildflower B&B Romance Series
Island Refuge
Island Dreams
Island Christmas
Island Hope

Contemporary Inspirational Romance Collection
In Love and War

Contemporary Novellas
Brewed with Love
Sara's Gift

Made in the USA
Middletown, DE
01 June 2020